Visions of Knight

A.D. Fletcher

Jacob's Ladder Series

Book 2

Dedication

To those labeled as different, strange, odd or a freak - don't let others words define you. Rejoice in being yourself, because we are not meant to fit in the molds that others create for us.

A special thanks goes to Kelly, Kim, Sean, Sue and the rest of my extended family.

Cover Art

Karl Dahmer at Dahmer Art

So the story continues...

Jenny stands in the her room dripping dry with her towel wrapped around her torso reading the note over and over. All I can do is sit on her bed holding the four daggers baffled at what's happening.

It's been less than an hour since we left the others and maybe three hours since I hacked a Sumerian god to death with an ax.

Jenny snaps her fingers in my face to get my attention and bring me back to reality and she says, "Hello, are you even listening to me?"

Shaking off the fog my head was currently in I say, "What did you say? Sorry this has just been a hell of a few weeks."

Jenny hands me the note back and begins to dry off, her naked body just a foot away causing me to almost lose focus again. As she dries off she says, "I said, who are these Knights twelve and what do you have that belongs to them?"

I rub my temples and try to think over what they could possibly want and say, "Honestly? I have no clue, I mean you've seen my place. I don't have much at all really and sure as shit nothing that could or would've belonged to some sort of knights." I set three of the daggers on the bed and look over the forth. It looks ordinary enough to me but I'm no expert on bladed weapons. The knife I usually carry I got on sale for less than ten bucks at the superstore.

Jenny now clothed comes over and picks up one of the daggers to get a better look. After examining the weapon she says, "I've seen this type of knife in a few movies before. You know the ones with knights and crusaders and stuff. Do you think these are the real deal?"

Still checking out the dagger for any distinguishing marks I say, "Probbly not, they would be worth a pretty penny if they were. We can always hope, I could use the extra cash."

Snatching the dagger out of my hand she says, "You can't pawn them. We should keep them, they could come in handy later on."

There was a knock on the front door, without thinking I grab a dagger of the bed and hurry to the door. Yanking the door open, knife in hand I find a Hispanic teenage male holding two bags of food. Holding the knife to my side I say, "Who sent you?"

Jenny pushes me out of the way and hands him cash and says, "I ordered food, remember?" Taking one of the bags from him she hands it to me. As she takes the second bag she hands him a few extra dollars saying, "Sorry, here's extra for your tip." She closes the door as he walks away and Jenny makes her way into another room with the food, so I follow her.

Never being in her house before I find myself moving slower than Jenny. I look around at the shelves full of books, movies, music, and I notice all of her furniture matches. I catch myself wondering why she would be with someone like me.

Hell other than the earth shattering sex I really don't have much to offer, then I hear her yell from the next room, "You do remember I can hear your thoughts, right? Get in here with the food, I think you have my order."

"Shit, sorry. I'm coming." I head into what I find out is the kitchen and hand her the bag. She already has plates out and was dividing the food up between us when I get in there. "I swear I need to start making notes or something. Too much new shit to remember."

Opening the last container she says, "That's no joke. Just so you know I try to stay out of your mind, it's a mess up there." Jenny hands me my plate and I follow her to the couch.

She turns on the TV with the remote and the first thing we see is a news report showing the empty lot across from my apartment building. There's cops everywhere taking statements and roping off the area. The reporter is saying that the gas company has been alerted and is checking for a leak in the area.

Something about the witnesses stories not matching up. I can understand that because there is no house there now or any sign that there was one. That and the fact that people were describing a giant with bull legs and dragon arms attacking a man swinging a large bone club. I'm pretty sure I wouldn't buy that story either if I wasn't there in the middle of it.

She seemed as sick of it as I was from the way she changed the channel. We ate quietly for a few minutes and I knew what she was thinking and she was right. I say, "I'll get hold of Mother after we eat and see what they know about the whole Knights thing."

Jenny smiled while she was getting ready to take a bite and says, "Good idea, I'll get my laptop and see if I can find anything on the internet." There's no way to know if it was her telling me to do it or if I just gave off that vibe but by the way she was smiling I'm guessing she had something to do with it.

We finished eating and I took the plates back to the kitchen. I tossed the containers in the trash and picked up the dagger off of the counter. Pulling my phone out of my pocket I snap a few pictured and text them to Sebastian.

Flipping the dagger as I walked back to the couch texting the details of the note to Sebastian I hear Jenny say something but can't make out what it is. As I come around the corner without looking up I say, "Hey babe, did you say something?"

"You remember Sarah, don't you?" Jenny says causing me to look up and not pay attention to where the knife was. It fell from my hand and stuck straight into the hardwood floor. I start to reach out to shake her hand to say hello when Jenny's voice comes through clearly in my head, "Your arms."

Looking down I realize what she means. There's no human flesh left only the black onyx like demigod shell and I quickly put my arms behind my back. Jenny covers for me and says, "He got into something while doing maintenance where he works, fiberglass everywhere. He already hugged me twice and I had to shower to get that stuff off me or I was going to itch my skin off."

Sarah pulls her hand back and says, "It's cool, just sit in that chair over there. I live on the couch half the time and don't want to worry about itching." Sarah starts to head up stairs toward her room and stops two steps up and say, "Real quick, why were you juggling a large knife?"

I look at the dagger that's buried at least an inch and a half into the floor and say, "No reason, I found it cleaning out and apartment and Jenny thought it was cool and wanted it."

Seeming satisfied with my answer Sarah continues her way upstairs. Jenny shot me a dirty look and says, "We have to be more careful, or we're going to have to tell her the truth. I'm not sure she can take it just yet. So tomorrow we go get you more clothes."

"Damn it." I protest. "I hate clothes shopping. Haven't I been through enough already?"

Without bothering to pander to my resistance Jenny says, "We should probably get you some gloves as well."

"Fine." I say with disdain. "Whatever you say, babe."

"Damn right, whatever I say." Jenny says with a grin. "Now if you would, please get the dagger out of the floor and get over here, it's movie time."

I pull the dagger from the floor with a swift yank and make my way to the chair Sarah has assigned me to. It took me only a few seconds sitting in this thing to realize that either Sarah hates me or she has never sat in this thing. It has got to be the most uncomfortable thing ever created. I think the Geneva Convention has outlawed objects such as this chair. The wood creaks at the slightest movement, while the so-called padding was as firm as a slab of concrete. I can't take the torment any longer and stood up. I look around the room spotting a pillow. I grab the pillow and throw it on the floor in front of the couch in front of Jenny. I plop down on the pillow, leaning back against the couch and rest the back of my head on Jenny's legs.

Jenny scrolls through the movie list and settles on some period movie about knights. It's not something that I would've picked but it doesn't take me too long to get hooked. The way the knights were portrayed as honorable, valiant, and fighting for the underdog. This makes my mind wander, what could I have that makes them come after me here? How would a group of knights know what I am, when I just found out myself a week ago?

I'm not sure how long I was lost in thought, but I was literally zapped back to reality by Jenny's touch. I can feel the electric tingle transfer as she runs her fingers across my neck.

Jenny lets out a giggle and says, "I think I'm getting the hang of the having a gift thing."

Turning towards her, now on my knees I lean close and say, "You know, you're going to need to be careful with that teasing stuff. If you think it's going to be hard to explain the black, stone-like skin to your friend, just wait till I'm glowing."

She pushes me back and smugly says, "You're right, I guess that means you're cut off. Well at least till we get your place livable again."

I slide my pillow to the far side of the floor on the other end of the couch and sit out of her reach. Crossing my arms I say, "Well, I know what I'm doing first thing tomorrow. That place will be finished in no time flat, those Knight people are going to need to wait."

Jenny nudges me with her foot and says, "You can do that after we go shopping. Now shut up and watch the movie."

"Well shit." I mumble under my breath. Jenny taps me with her foot again and points to the TV.

My phone vibrates in my pocket. I pull it out and see I got a message from Sebastian. Once I open it I read "KEEP THE SHOTGUN CLOSE. NEVER LET IT OUT OF YOUR SIGHT." It being all in caps I figure I should do what he says. I'm sure he has his reasons.

I get up from the floor and start heading upstairs to grab the shotgun from Jenny's room. Jenny looks up and says, "Where you going, babe?"

Not wanting to say what I'm doing out loud where Sarah might hear I say, "Just got to go grab something, I'll be right back."

Laying her head back down she says, "Okay, grab the blanket out of my chair when you come back."

Giving her a thumbs up, I make my way up stairs and say, "I'm on it."

I open the door to Jenny's room and head to the bed where I tossed my hoodie earlier. I remember wrapping the shotgun up in my hoodie before I got in the shower. I pull it out of my hoodie and I feel relief that it's still safe. Just to make sure that it's safe in her room I set it down and check the windows to see if they are locked. Everything appears locked and sealed up. Before heading back down stairs I make a pit stop in the restroom. I'm being quiet so I don't bother her roommate.

I hear a door open on this floor and footsteps heading down towards Jenny's room. I reach over and swing the bathroom door closed as quietly as I could. I hear Sarah talking but it's hard to understand what's being said through the walls.

I finish up in the bathroom and stand there for a minute when I see through the cracked door, Sarah enter Jenny's bedroom. My onyx skin exposed on my arms causes me to not make an abrupt entrance and startle her, so I wait.

From my hiding spot I hear her say, "I have them. Do you want me to snag all 4 of them." There was a moment of silence, I'm assuming while she waited on the callers response. Then she says, "Okay, the 3 is good for now. I will get that other thing as well."

The thought hits me, she's talking about the daggers and my gun. I jerk the door open and dart into the room saying, "DROP IT!"

I startle Sarah, causing her to drop her phone and a box of condoms on the floor as she spun around to face me. In her right hand she still held a bottle of massage oil. Still freaked out, and now mad Sarah says, "What the hell? You just scared the shit out of me."

I hear Jenny running up the stairs and down the hallway in our direction. Jenny enters the room to find Sarah staring at me. I know she's looking at the exposed onyx-like flesh of my arms from her frightened expression. Jenny went to Sarah's side, rubbing her back to help her calm down says, "What's going on in here?"

I spoke first to give Sarah a chance to catch her breath saying, "First off, I'm sorry for scaring you. After the last few days things have made me a little edgy. Second, I heard her on the phone while I was in the bathroom. She was saying something about taking 3 and couldn't get the forth as well as getting something else. I didn't know she meant you know, condoms."

Sarah turns to Jenny showing a mix of humiliation and anger and says, "I was on the phone getting ready for my date and after you said he was covered in itchy stuff I figured I could raid you stash and get you more before you needed them. That was till your freak of a boyfriend came bursting in here like SWAT."

Jenny trying to keep the peace in the room says, "He's not a freak, just different. He apologized, so lets just move on. I'm sure he's really sorry." Jenny points at me as if it was my cue to apologize again.

Putting my hands together to plead forgiveness I say, "I truly am sorry. I shouldn't have burst in here the way I did."

Sarah still fuming, says in an angry tone, "Look at him, freak. I'm surprised he's even house broken. I told you that night at the bar to drop him then."

Jenny embarrassed by her saying that, turned away to hide her face. I couldn't take this any longer. I grab my clothes off the bed and take off Karl's shirt, putting mine back on. Grabbing my hoodie, shotgun and the daggers I say, "I know when I'm not wanted around. This is both or your place, not mine. I'm out."

Ignoring Jenny's pleas to stay, I continue down the stairs and out the front door. The closed front door muffles the voices coming from inside. I think it's safer this way, not just for Jenny and Sarah but for me as well. I've survived for years without anyone watching my back, at least now my back is bulletproof. With Sebastian having my work truck, it left me on foot.

I cut across the neighbors yard and duck into the shadows, just in time to avoid Jenny from seeing me. I hear her and Sarah yelling my name, begging me to come back. They gave up after a few minutes and I knew when Jenny got in her car and drove off, it was safe for me to make my move.

With a tear in my eye, I turned my phone off and started walking. I had no destination in mind, it was more just to walk. I use to be good at finding a safe place to crash. Hours must have passed, wandering the streets and alleyways avoiding peoples glances. When I got tired of walking I stopped to look around to get my baring, and the answer was right in front of me.

I guess somehow I knew where I was going the whole time. My body took me home, right to the back of my apartment building. My apartment was in no way inhabitable right now with all the bodies laying around, but my first place was.

Making my way up the flights of stairs as stealthy as I can in this creaky old building, I stop randomly to listen for anyone following and peek out windows to check for any cars out of place. Finally to the attic door, I check it for any signs that someone else might have tampered with it. Everything looks normal, so I enter.

The faint moonlight showing through the broken window wasn't enough light to see the entire room, but it will be plenty to see to get to the matches and light a candle or two. I close the door behind me and use the daggers to jam into the frame. This gives me a little peace of mind knowing that nobody was getting in this door without a battering ram.

Inching my way through the room to where I remember putting the matches, I almost trip on the stool that Jenny had used earlier. I find the first candle in the corner and trace it with my hand to find the base where I left the matches, no luck. With what happened between Jenny and I there is a chance they got knocked to the floor.

Kneeling down I run my hand across the floor searching for the matches. I hear movement in the room and remember I left the shotgun by the door. Slowly making my way to where I set it still acting like I'm looking for the matches. Reaching the shotgun with my left hand, I pick it up gently and turn towards the direction of the noise. Aiming from the hip I place my finger on the trigger.

There was a flash and then I felt as if something hit me in the chest hard. The blast sent me flying backwards and out the already broken window. As I fly back the anticipation of impact sets in as the fall increases. Knowing the attic is at least fives stories up and the distance I was launched away from the building, I know I'm about to eat pavement.

I come to, finding Jenny sobbing next to me. I hear her crying, her hands covering her face. Forcing my neck to work, I look around and realize I'm embedded in a cars roof. I reach up and touch her hand causing her to gasp. Trying to let her know I'm okay I say, "Babe, you take my breathe away."

Her tear streaming eyes quickly changed from sadness to anger. Jenny grabs my hoodie and begins shacking me and says, "I thought I killed you, asshole. Why did you leave?"

Getting my baring back I push myself up from the roof of some poor bastards 1980's Bonneville. As I attempt to swing my legs around so I can get down I say, "Well, if you let me get down we can talk about it. I did just fly through a car from five stories up."

Jenny lets go of her death grip on my hoodie and says, "Fine, give me your hand." As our hands combine, I feel a pulse of energy hit me. Instantly I'm good as new.

Once my feet were on the ground , I stretch and say, "Lets get up stairs where we can talk. Also I don't want to be around when the owner of this car shows up and sees this mess."

While we walked back upstairs to my attic Jenny was occasionally bumping me, causing me to hit the wall. We had to duck under a few pieces of police tape. My apartment in the moon light looks like something out of a horror movie. Blood splatter covering the walls and even some on the ceiling. Creeping through my marked off apartment, we carefully snoop around for any of the books they might have missed while bagging evidence.

The books, scrolls and maps were all still there. The only thing missing was the notepad that has my dream written on it. I pick up one of the downed curtains from the floor and lay it out flat. Jenny and I stack all of the research material in the middle. Tying the corners together I heave the bundle over my shoulder and start for the door. We make our way to the next flight when we see flashlights shinning down the hall.

We stop in the shadows and listen for a moment as a mail voice says, "Unit 816 to dispatch."

There was a pause then the male says, "Hey dispatch, it appears someone has been in this unit recently. We are going to enter and search the area."

I send Jenny up the stairs on her own to get the door open and wait for me. I gently swing the bundle of books of my shoulder so I can carry it in front and not worry about accidentally hitting a wall or light fixture as I go up the stairs. As gingerly as I can move, I take each step a delicately as possible. Getting into the room, I set the books on the mattress and secure the door with the daggers.

Knowing we aren't out of the woods yet we remain very still. Foot steps sound on the attic stairs, causing my heartbeat to pound harder and harder. The light from the officers flashlight began streaming through seams of the door. I motion for Jenny to back up away from in front of the door and I do the same. Moving as nimble as we can among the piles of long forgotten junk was providing more difficult than anticipated.

The handle jiggled as the officer tried the door. The knob turns but the door doesn't budge in the slightest. With the amount of times he is trying, he must really want in here. He even slammed into it with the handle turned but the blades held in place. When the slamming stopped I knew it wasn't over. The light swept back and forth under the door, like he was trying to see inside through the one inch crack. Jenny's eye caught mine and I hear her voice in my head saying, "Good idea on backing up." I acknowledge her with a nod.

When the light finally went away and the creaks of the floorboards grew distant, we held our spots silently. The waiting was becoming tiresome and beginning to wear on us both. Looking into her eyes from across this tiny room, I knew I hurt her by walking out. I hear the squad cars siren chirp through the broken window and fade off as they drive away.

Not wanting to waste another second in two large steps I hold her in my arms. Tucking my head into the crook of her neck I softly say, "I'm sorry I walked out. I thought it was for the best. I did it to keep you safe."

She leans back and takes my head in her hands, looking me in the eyes and ,says "You were told before, you aren't allowed to think on your own. I love you and no matter what that bitch says it won't change that. First off, I see how well you can take care of yourself. Another thing, who needs four condoms for one date?"

I kiss her and say, "I know I'm a dumbass and I don't think at times. I thought that you would be safer without me there and I didn't want to screw up anything for you and Sarah."

She smiles and says, "See that's what you get for thinking."

I loosen my grip around her and slide my hands to her hips and say, "Oh, what the hell was that anyway. I point a gun in the dark and you shoot me with a ball of light out the window and into a car."

Holding her hands up to her side she says, "I don't know how to turn it on and off. It just happens, like some kind of defensive thing. I will try not to do it again."

Rubbing my chest where the thing hit me I say, "Good, cause that shit hurt."

Jenny covers her mouth to cover her laughter, I pull her hand away and kiss her more deeply. We let go of each other and look around the room knowing we were stuck in for the night, not wanting to chance that one of the officers stayed behind.

I take the curtain that I used for a book tote and look for a way to tack it up into the hole where the window once was. I see a few rusty nails jutting out from the remaining frame. Pushing the nail through the fabric till it tears, hooking the corners. It's not the prettiest job, but it will block the candle light from escaping and painting a target on our hiding spot. While I dealt with the window, Jenny was sliding boxes in front of the door to block any potential viewer.

I power my phone up and use the light to look for the matches. Once it is fully on it begins vibrating non stop. I flip it over and watch as the messages pile up one after another. Looking at Jenny I say, "Damn, how many texts did you send me? My battery will be dead before I can read them all."

Not looking up from a box she was digging through she says, "Ummm, a lot. But you can disregard the last twenty or so. They go from angry to violent after the first five."

Shaking my head in amazement of how long it's been going I turn my cell to silent to stop it from vibrating and use the light from the screen on the floor near the candle. It took a minute to finally find them, excited to get some light going in the room I light the first candle.

Using the candle I make my way around the room to light the rest. I stop to see what Jenny has found, since she seems so engrossed in these old boxes. Setting the candle down to give her light in the corner I say, "What kind of junk did you find that has you so interested over here?"

With the dust thick in the air from her rummaging , she hands me a stack of old photographs and says, "I think I found something. Here, take a look at these."

Flipping through a few of them I say, "So what, just some old pictures of some women."

Smacking my arm Jenny says, "Are you that dense? Look, and I mean really look."

I wipe the dust on the first couple pictures on my pant leg. Moving closer to the candle, I examine the first one and with confusion I say, "Is that...... is that Mother? Who the hell is she with?"

Jenny snatches the picture from my hand and flips it over. There is faded writing that's hard to make out in the candles dim glow. Jenny tires of my attempts to see what she is pointing out says "4th of July celebration, Catherine Hess and Mother 1943."

As I stare at the image, a feeling of dread and bewilderment flows over me. In complete disbelief I say, "That can't be right. 1943? She looks the exact same here as she does now."

Jenny hands me more pictures saying, "Right? She's the same in all of these too. They date back to 1919. See, baby Catherine 1919."

I spread the pictures out, trying to get them in order by date I say, "I think this Catherine person is the old lady downstairs. If I'm right, that would mean Mother is over a hundred and hasn't aged a day."

My stomach turns, not knowing what to think of this revelation. Being connected to Jenny psychically makes it hard to hide what I'm feeling. She leans over to me wrapping her arm over my shoulder says, "Maybe she didn't tell you to protect you."

Looking them over, my thoughts race with the possibilities of why and I say, "Yeah, I guess. There's no way to know without asking."

Jenny kisses me on the cheek as her way of letting me know she's here for me. I give her a little half hug as a thank you. I look for where I set my phone at so I can snap a few pictures. Seeing the message light blink on the phone, I lean back to try to reach it without getting up. Realizing it's just out of reach, I get up and walk over to where I left it by the chair.

Bending over and grabbing it, I hit the button to turn on my screen and see I have 9 voice mails and 37 text messages. Glancing up to see Jenny I say, "Damn, girl. 9 voice mails and 37 text, I don't think I've ever had that many in one day before."

Jenny still digging through boxes says, "Hey, that's not all me. I only left one voice mail. As for the text, at most twenty-five."

Now intrigued by who might have been trying to get hold of me, I unlock the phone. I got to the text screen to see who else they were from and say ,"A few from Sebastian and a few from another number."

Jenny came over to see and says, "That's strange, no name just a number. What do they say?" She taps the screen and the messages pop open.

As they open we see they are from Fred. From how they were stated they were urgent. One after the other saying to hide and not come out until we receive word. One said that they tried reaching Jenny and can't, so they hope she is safe with me.

Hoping Sebastian's messages went into more detail, I check those. More of the same things that Fred had sent. That there's no time to explain and to get somewhere that we could hide out for a while. Checking the voice mails I see they are they same.

I text Fred and Sebastian that we were safe, not saying where, just that we were hiding out. I let Sebastian know I had questions that need answers and soon. Setting my phone down, I knew all we could do is wait.

Worn thin from the days activities, sleep moved up on the list of things to do. Jenny and I both yawn in unison as we fix the makeshift bed, so we can be more comfortable. Jenny remembers that there were a few blankets in one of the boxes. Spreading them out, the floor almost resembles a bed.

Keeping the shotgun close, we made an attempt at sleeping. With Jenny at my side, the images of my dreams jump around, making it hard to pinpoint where and when things were happening. The clothes and surroundings change, finally settling. Armored horses being lead by young boys wearing things I've seen on fliers for the Renaissance festival. Iron clad knights walking the packed streets. The aroma of filth fills the air.

Sticking to the shadows and edges of the road, I make my way cautiously through the town. The bellow of the trumpets causes the crowds to split, opening the road for a convoy of men on horseback leading the way. All the men flew a flag with a field of white with a red cross in the middle.

As the knights pass, a gold embossed carriage came into view. To improve my view, I shift to a nearby alleyway. Using a wooden crate, I stand on it to see over the crowd. Curious of who was so important that they need a golden carriage with this much muscle as an escort I try to catch a glimpse of the passenger through the flapping velvet curtains. If by fate, the wind picks up as the carriage is directly in my line of sight. The velvet parts revealing Jenny.

I try to get a better look, afraid my eyes are playing tricks on me, and the wind calms. I have to know for sure if it is her. Skirting the wall behind the crowds of people, I managed to move unnoticed. All attention was on the riders and carriage. Flowers were being tossed in the street as cheering fills the air.

Getting more bold, I pick up speed as the parade does. Losing focus on where I'm going I stumble over a basket of apples someone had set back out of their way. Reaching for anything as I fall, without looking I feel my hand grip cloth. Picking myself up from the ground I notice the cloth was the tail of a mans tunic.

The furious man turns, I see the same white with red cross on the front of his tunic. As he sees my face the man yells, "It's him, guards seize him!"

Another man yells, "Surround the Princess! Don't allow him to escape!"

In the confusion of the crowd, I duck through the people, staying as low as possible. Seeing an opening, I dart between two of the guards into an alley. Once I reach open ground I run as fast as my legs will carry me. After a few twists and turns, I slow my pace to a jog and then to a walk. I grab a shroud from a window as I pass by. Covering my head as I walk, I begin to blend into the people in the marketplace.

I feel safe, hidden in plain sight. A passersby gives me a nod, and I return the gesture out of courtesy. All seems normal until I hear a man scream, "It's the prince! He's over here!"

I turn and see the man I exchanged nods with pointing at me. Spinning to run again, the last thing I see is the shield as it makes contact with the left side of my face.

I awaken in a sweat, being shaken by Jenny. Sitting up quickly I say, "I'm up, I'm up."

Jenny sitting next to me, rubbing my back as I shake the cobwebs loose says, "Are you okay? You were moving around a lot in your sleep."

Shifting to face her I say, "I guess I'm alright. I had the craziest dream, or memory, hell I don't know what it was."

She places a hand on my cheek and asks, "Were there knights, crowds and stuff? If so, I had the same one."

Feeling like an idiot for even thinking differently I say, "Oh yeah, the entire linked thing. At least you didn't get smashed in the face with a shield. I wish I knew why those guys were after me.

She leans back against a stack of boxes and says, "Hey, you may have been chased and hit, but I was chained up in that carriage. I kept being told that I should be happy to be marrying the new king. Something about it's the will of the church."

Thinking for a moment I say, "Well, the church thing makes sense with the whole cross wearing knights, but not sure about the other stuff. The marriage to the king is kind of trippy considering I got called a prince and you a princess."

The morning sun peers in between the wall and my half ass curtain job, shining directly on the blades of the daggers. Shielding my eyes from the glare, I get up to remove the curtain to give us more light in our hiding spot. Tossing the curtain to the side, I decide I should check our door. The daggers were dug in deep into the wooden frame.

As I wiggle the dagger, the details begin to stand out. Not sure if it's from the dream, or looking at them with rested eyes, but the symbol on the butt of the handle is more pronounced. The red cross was a mosaic of what might be ruby. The white that surrounded it could be ivory. Checking the other three daggers, I notice they are all matching blades. I call Jenny over, pointing out the detail to her.

Propping myself up I look out the window trying to get a view of the street, hoping not to see any sign of cops. The normal cars line the street, nothing seems out of place. I check my phone for the time, I see it's still early. Standing with my hands on my hips, I try to decide what our options are. I look at Jenny and say, "I don't know about you, but I'm getting hungry. While we're out, we can get some provisions for when we are in lock down. Sound good to you?"

Jenny seeming a little skeptical of my idea says, "I thought we were supposed to hide, and not come out until they tell us."

Gathering a few of the pictures up I say, "Well yeah, but we have no food, and without any power our phones will be dead and we won't know when it's safe to come out."

Jenny grabs her bag and heads the door and says, "Good point, I want waffles." Then she pulls the daggers from the door and sticks them one by one in her bag.

I try hurrying, since our door is no longer barricaded. Tying the sling tighter for the shotgun, I slip it over my shoulder, and put my hoodie on. I check one more time to see if I had everything before walking out the door, then we left.

We made our way quietly down the stairs, being careful not to draw unwanted attention to ourselves. As we cleared a few floors, we started relax a little. One more set of stairs and we will be home free. I was the first to step through the threshold to the outside, and is abruptly stopped by the back end of a massive flashlight. My eyes followed the flashlight to see who was holding it, and am not surprised to find officer friendly from Jacqueline's store.

Keeping the flashlight in my chest, the officer says, "Hey, I remember you. Didn't I see you at the break in at the bookstore the other day?"

Careful not to draw attention to my side where the shotgun hangs, I turn slightly to show him I wasn't alone and say, "Yeah, that was me, small city. What's going on?"

Digging the base of the light into my sternum the officer says, "I thought so, I don't think it's a coincidence that you just show up at two different crime scenes. What are you doing here, punk?"

I don't want him to know that the jabs to the chest don't hurt, so I play it off like they do. Rubbing my chest I say, "Crime scene, what crime scene? We're just here visiting my great aunt Catherine for a few days."

Agitated by my answer the officer jabs me once more and says, "Great-aunt, you say. Well, lets just go check with this Catherine, an see if your story is true.

Shrugging my shoulders I ask, "Okay, do you want me to lead or follow you up there?"

The officer shoves me back and says, "You lead, smartass."

I pass Jenny on the stairs and lead the way, certain that he won't touch her the way he does me. Once we make it to the forth floor, I move a little faster so I could knock on the door first before he could. Banging on the door a few times as he shows up, the door opens.

Hoping she catches on I say, "Aunt Catherine, would you please let this officer know that we have been staying here? Mother is waiting on us and we need to hurry, you know how she gets when she is kept waiting."

The officer pushes me to the side and says, "Do you know these two? I caught them leaving the building. This entire area is a crime scene."

Mrs. Hess adjusts her glasses, and says, "Jacob, Jenny, you two run along. You shouldn't keep your mother waiting, she be worried sick." Waving Jenny and I off she says, "Don't forget to get the milk on your way home. Now what did you need officer?"

I tap Jenny on the shoulder to go, and say, "Okay Auntie, I will. Sorry to waste your time officer." I follow Jenny, scooting behind him as we head down the hallway towards the stairs.

The moment we made it to the third floor, we picked up the pace. Jenny and I made record time clearing the last few floors. We make it to the street, and I follow Jenny to her car.

I look over the outside of the car, to see if there is any sign of tampering. Nothing external that I can see, but it's good to be cautious since we have no clue what we are up against. Jenny fires up the car, and off we go. She suggests going to a place she knows for breakfast that's away from our area. Maybe we will run less of a chance of coming in contact with the people looking for us.

I know she said this place was out of the way, but I wasn't expecting a truck stop diner. The food was better than I thought it was going to be, and they had plugs right at the table to charge your phone while you eat. The great thing about truck stops is that they have almost every item you could possibly need, and tons of other shit you don't.

We eat our breakfast, did a little shopping for a few necessary supplies. You know, the crap that you see and say, "Oh my God, I can't live without this in my life", and never touch again. I really should be kept on a shorter leash, but that's beside the point. Jenny found me a good, lightweight, baggie, long sleeve shirt to help conceal the shot gun, while covering my onyx skin. While she did that, I check out their glove selection, settling on a pair of black, leather riding gloves.

On our way out, I check my phone, no response from Fred or Sebastian. Not having too many options, I run back in and grab a gallon of 2% milk for Catherine. Showing the milk to Jenny as I get back in the car, she knew where we were heading.

We arrive back at the apartment building, circling the block once before committing to a spot. It's also a good way to find out if we are being followed, seems safe from a tail or cop cars. The thought crosses my mind as we park down the street. When we left, I didn't see a cop car around but he was certainly there waiting as we walked out.

Jenny either was reading my mind, or was having the same thoughts, because as she gets out of the car, she seems more anxious than usual. Feeling her anxiety, I come around to her side of the car, pull her close, and kiss her before she can say a word. I feel her relax, as her muscles unclench in my arms and then I ask, "Better?"

She nods yes, and locks the car doors. I slip the shotgun off my shoulder and hand it to her saying, "Here, you take this and give me two of the daggers. I'm going to go first, and you keep this tucked away until it's needed."

Jenny agrees, and I slide two of the daggers in the back of my pants, fix my shirt and grab the supplies. We move steadily, but cautious on the approach to the building. Looking around, I don't see the officer from earlier. Acting as casual as we can, I take that first step into the building.

Sparks fly, as the tazer is buried in my side. The electricity pulses, not having the desired effect on me. Turning my head, I see Officer Friendly with his arm fully extended trying to keep as far back as he can, and still reach me. Surprise fills his face when I'm not dropping to the ground. The blue glow of my skin gets brighter, the longer he holds that trigger.

I reach up for his arm a moment too late. A flash comes from behind me, causing him to fly backwards against the wall, smacking his head on the light fixture, leaving his slumped body on the floor.

My thoughts immediately go to Mrs. Hess. Not waiting to see if Friendly was still breathing, I dart up the stairs as fast as I can move, with Jenny close behind. As I hit the 4th floor I had a dagger out an ready. Looking back I see Jenny, she has the shotgun out and is watching to see if we have anyone following.

Banging on the door hard, I wait for a moment for her to answer. After waiting for a moment of not getting a response, I take a step back to get enough room to kick in the door. As I kick, the door opens. Trying to stop from planting my foot in the middle of the nice ladies chest, I step wide, losing my balance.

Jenny rushes over to see why I fell, and finds the wonderful widow standing in the doorway, staring at me on the floor. So happy she was okay, Jenny hugs her. Mrs. Hess was truly confused by this, but hugs her back.

Getting off the floor, I say, "I'm glad you're okay."

Not knowing why we are so concerned with her well-being all of the sudden Mrs. Hess says, "Of course I'm alright, why wouldn't I be?"

Adjusting my clothes from the fall, I ask, "Do you mind if we come in, it might take a minute to explain, and I think it might be safer if we didn't do it in the hallway."

Stepping to the side, Mrs. Hess says, "Well, that depends. Did you remember the milk?"

I look around for where I set them down at, and pick up the two jugs to show her and say, "Yes, yes ma'am I did." With a smile, she waves us into her apartment.

As I walk through the doorway, I notice that the door frame on the inside was made of some sort of stone. There were several other anomalies that stood out as well, sigils painted on the floor and ceiling that were barely visible, an old tapestry hanging on the back of the door. Gazing around the room, I see the book shelves are cluttered with occult literature and items.

We all sit. The thought that Mrs. Hess is deeper into my hidden reality than I ever knew someone could be crosses my mind, so I say, "Mrs. Hess, what's up with all of the occult stuff? I know you said you know Mother and all, but exactly how much do you know about me?"

Clapping her hands Mrs. Hess says, "First things first child, what was all that mess with the officer? Are you in some kind of trouble? He was very insistent."

Leaning back on the couch, I say, "Honestly, we don't know. That was only the second time seeing him before, and the third time was just a few minutes ago. That wasn't a very pleasant time either."

Listening intently she asks, "Really, why's that?"

"Well, as I came in the door to the building, he zapped me with one of those stun guns. If Jenny wouldn't have been there, who knows what would have happened. That's why we rushed up here, we thought he might have tried to hurt you or something." I say.

Mrs. Hess picks up a tea cup from her end table and takes a sip, as she sets it down says, "It's awfully nice of you to worry about me, but he couldn't get in here if he wanted to, nobody can. You see, thanks to some things Mother gave me over the years, I'm safe and sound."

Jenny sits forward a little and says, "We haven't met yet and he didn't seem to feel the need to introduce me." Jenny looks over her shoulder at me before continuing, "I'm Jenny, this ones girlfriend."

With a little snicker Mrs. Hess says, "Oh child, I know who you are. In fact, I not only know who you both are, but what you are. It makes me happy that you found each other."

Her statement made us both sit up at attention and simultaneously say, "WHAT!" The surprise in our voice came out louder than expected.

Picking her tea cup up, Mrs. Hess says, "Oh, calm down you two. There's so much I can tell you, but it will take some time." Getting up from her chair, Mrs. Hess slowly made her way to her bookcase. Looking shelf to shelf, she retrieved a rather large book.

Returning to her seat, she set the book on her lap and says, "You need to promise me something before we get into all this."

There was no option but to do as she asks so I say, "Sure, anything."

Flipping open the book, she begins scanning the pages and says, "You need to get me a new television, after the two of you going at it the other day, all that electricity fried mine. Because of you two, I'm missing my shows."

More than a little embarrassed Jenny's head drops, I say, "I am so sorry. Yes I will definitely get you a new TV."

Looking up from the book she says, "Great, now we can start. Well, my family are sort of record keepers. We document the lives of the, I think Mother calls them gifted. Somewhere down the line my family was chosen to record your story."

Interested and confused I say, "My story, you mean my family lineage, right?"

She must have understood my confusion, because she replies, "No, my dear. Just the two of you. Every lifetime we wait to see if you find each other, and you can't understand how happy it makes me that I get to see it in my life."

This perks Jenny right up and into the conversation as she says, "Lifetime, how many have there been, and are you saying we are meant to be together?"

Almost ecstatic to explain Mrs. Hess says, "Oh you are most definitely meant to be together. Together you two make a whole, in all the recordings there have only been four times, I think, that you were able to come close. Oh, they do their best to keep you apart. That's why you were placed with those nice people as a baby."

Feeling lost, and not knowing what to think, I say, "Mother mentioned that they weren't my parents before, but who are the 'they' you were talking about, and why keep us apart?"

Passing me the book Mrs. Hess says, "The 'they', well that changes with the generations. You never know till it happens really. Once it was the church, there were a few of the other gods, kings, governments. They each have their own agenda, but I guess it either boils down to jealousy or fear or the power that you two combined hold."

Sitting back, feeling overwhelmed with all this knowledge that was just dropped on us, I say, "I don't know what to say. I mean I'm a maintenance man, and she delivers Italian food. If we are so important, why hasn't anyone told us this before?"

Sounding a little ashamed she says, "For one thing, we aren't supposed to get involved, just sit back and record what happens. For another, it could hinder the outcome of it all, but you two are together now so it doesn't matter. Can I see it?"

Not knowing what she's talking about I say, "See what?"

Smiling she says, "The skin of the gods, silly."
A little shocked that she asked, and sort of embarrassed of it, it took me a moment to process whether or not to do it. Scooting forward on the couch, I placed the daggers on the table in front of me and unzips my hoodie. Before I took it off I say, "Are you sure, it's kinda odd looking?"

Mrs. Hess shook her head yes and says, "No reason to be child, with the things I've seen over the years, it won't bother me. I just want to know if the stories are true."

I slide my left arm out of the sleeve, and then my right. Her eyes lit up when my hardened, black skin came into view. Slowly she reaches forward, then stops and looks up at me, as if to ask if it's okay for her to touch it. I nod yes, and she continues her reach.

Carefully, her fingers trace the contours of my arm. Drawing her hand back, her smile faded, and replaced with sadness. Her eyes weld up with tears, confusing Jenny and I. I quickly putting my hoodie on to hide my skin once more, Jenny went to Catherine's side.

Jenny rubbing Catherine's back says, "Are you okay, what's wrong?"

Over her tears Catherine says, "I'm fine, dear. Just overwhelmed with joy. My family has watch over you for hundreds of years, and I'm the first, and probably the last of my line to ever see it. With your skin evolved this far, so early in your life, it means that my work is almost complete. It's also said to be…. Never mind."

The way she stopped, I knew there was something we weren't being told. I'm getting really tired of not being told things. The frustration set in and causes me to blurt out, "Said to be what? You can't start a sentence like that and say never mind!"

Drying her tear stained cheeks, Catherine says, "I'm really not supposed to say, actually I'm not even supposed to be talking to you two about any of this. You two are such good kids, I just couldn't pass it up."

Jenny began tearing up at what Catherine had said, and says, "Awe, that's so sweet of you to say."

Catherine patting Jenny on the leg says, "What I wasn't supposed to say, can be taken many different ways. They say that when you both are fully evolved, you will be unstoppable and bring about the end of days."

Stunned, I flop back on the couch. As if I don't have enough on my plate to deal with, now I have to worry about bringing on the end of days. I get up from my spot and head to the door. As I grab the door knob, Jenny says, "Where are you going, it's not safe out there."

Not looking back, I open the door and say, "It's okay, I will be right back. You stay here, with Mrs. Hess. This will just take a sec."

Working my way down stairs, not even checking around corners, I get to the ground floor. Against the wall, I see Officer Friendly slowly making his way to his feet. Before I even realize I had moved, I have him pressed against the wall, with his feet dangling.

The fear and pain was evident in him, from his silent cries, pleading for mercy. With my anger building, I push harder. I hear a combination of bones snapping, and plaster crumbling to the floor as I say, "I'm going to ask you one time, and one time only, if I don't like your answer, I'm going to start removing pieces, got it?" His sobbing stops long enough to shake his head yes. Taking that as my go ahead to continue, I say, "Good, then lets begin with a few simple questions, then work up to the hard ones. First question, what's your name?"

With a snot bubble forming from his sobs and rapid breathing, the officer says, "Steven, Steven Hatch, sir."

I lower him a little, just enough for his feet to barely brush the floor. Seeing hope in his eyes I say, "Question number two, are you even a cop?"

Steven wipes his face with his sleeve and says , "Yes sir, I am."

Lowering him another inch, I hear the plaster crack more as I say, "See, now we're getting somewhere. So Steven, the cop, this is when the questions get harder. Why THE FUCK did you attack me?"

His eyes widened with the rise in my voice. Within seconds Steven says, "They made me do it."

My agitation level grew. I lowered him all the way to the floor, just to slam him back into the wall again before I say, "See, see, there it is again. That word, 'they'. Everyone assumes I know who 'they' is. This next is a two part question. If I don't get the answers I will choke you with your own entrails. Who is 'they', and how did they make you do anything?"

The hope drained from his eyes, like the color from his face. Taking a moment to get his words right, Steven finally says, "My Captain gave the order, they have my daughter." His body went limp as his tears began to flow all over again.

I realize that he is just a pawn in this whole thing and let go of his uniform shirt, allowing him to slump to the floor. Thinking I almost killed him for protecting his family shook me to the core. All that I know is that this did nothing but leave me with more questions than answers. As I pace the floor I say, "I don't even know your captain, why would he want you to go after me? They had to know I wouldn't go down without a fight."

Trying to pull himself together Steven sniffles and says, "I don't know, maybe to say you hit a cop. That way they could charge you with a felony and lock you up. His buddy runs the jail. They would have you right where they want you, whenever they decide."

Reeling from the load just dropped on me, I sort the questions out in my head before I say, "I get it, people hate me for a reason that they won't tell me, but I was happy keeping to myself. Hell, the only actual reason I have a phone is so my boss can call me with changes. Well that and ordering food." Stopping for a moment as I try to put the pieces together, when I say, "Is this captain of yours a religious man, you know, like does he wear a red cross and stuff? Do you know if he likes knights, or any of that mid-evil crap?"

Steven brushes the plaster off of his clothes, and out of his hair then says, "Him and his buddies are knights at the Renaissance festival, does that count?"

As the pieces come together in my head, I ask, "You've said him and his buddies twice now, how many of them are there?"

I could see Steven counting not only in his head but also on his fingers, mumbling names too low to hear, when he says, "Counting him, I think there's twelve of them. I might be off by one or two."

I pace as I think out loud. "So, there's twelve of them, give or take. They all dress and play knights, stop me if I get any of this wrong." I say pointing at Steven, before I continue, "They did something to your family to get you to attack me. Oh, and of course yesterday some group calling themselves the 'Knights Twelve' leave a nasty little note on my girlfriends door. If your boss is part of it, it would make sense that they knew where I might go."

Steven says, "I don't know anything about a note, I was just told to wait here for you. There's no telling how many people they have working for them. Any one of those people could have stuck a note on Jenny's door."

"Yeah, I guess you're right." I say, then it hits me. "I never said her name was Jenny." Whipping my head around I see him trying to sneak passed me, towards the door. Kicking my left leg back, he trips. I grab him by his shirt, yanking him back, causing him to slam hard against the wall. As I rush towards his falling body, I notice a red cross pendant hanging form a chain draped around his neck.

I plant my shoulder in his sternum, driving him deeper into the old plaster wall. I hold him up by his shirt with my right hand as I jerk the chain from his neck. Dangling the cross in front of his face, I say, "What did I say would happen if I didn't like your answer? Well you lied to me, and that I don't like."

Steven's eyes come into focus on the swinging cross being held three inches from his face. In a panic, his hands fumble on his belt for only a moment until he finds what he's searching for. The knife stabs through my shirt and jacket just below my armpit, but won't penetrate my black skin. Dropping my left arm, I trap his arm in place. With a quick upward thrust to his elbow, I hear the snap of his bone.

I release his arm, letting the broken, limp limb fall to his side. I can see Steven fading in and out of consciousness. While he's still lucid, I say, "I need you to tell your bosses." Either from fear or pain, possibly both, Steven collapses to the floor. Seeing him laying, blacked out on the floor, I say, "Well, I guess I better write it down for you."

Picking up Steven's knife from next to his limp body, I rip open his shirt and start carving two words, "BACK OFF." I dig through his pockets, finding his wallet and keys. Taking his ID out, I think knowing where to find him later could prove valuable, I put his wallet back in his pocket. I toss him on my shoulder and head outside to find his car. Hitting the lock button on the key fob, I hear a chirp two cars down.

Once to the car, I open the drivers door and lower his body into the seat. Reaching across him, I start the car and crank the air conditioner up to full blast to help him snap out of his current state, and slam the door.

On the way back up to Catherine's apartment, I stop on my floor to take a look at what remains of my apartment. In the light of day, the amount of blood stains and police line tape, would make even the most jaded of souls question their actions.

Floor to ceiling splatter in some areas, chunks of what once was one or multiple attackers in others. Looking in my bedroom, I see the blood soaked sheets containing my molted torso skin. The amount of blood from that night, turned my mattress into a sponge.

Most of my clothes have been ruined over the previous few weeks by either someone else's blood or my own. Going back to the living room I gather a few more books, scrolls, and other things I didn't want to leave behind. One more quick once over and I knew it was time to go.

I drop my spoils from the salvage in the attic and cover them with a dirty drop cloth, to help it remain hidden. Standing at Catherine's door, I knock a few times. Seeing the blood on my hands and sleeve from the interaction with Steven moments before, I tuck my hands quickly into my pockets to avoid the awkward questions.

The door opens and it's Jenny standing there. I'm not sure if it is relief I see in her welled up eyes of me coming back or if something else happened in my absence. She steps out into the hallway and as soon as she crossed the threshold, she smacked me hard right on the cheek, and immediately wraps her arms around me hugging me. I'm not a genius but I'm guessing it's the me coming back.

Still holding me tight, Jenny whispers in my ear, "If you pull that shit again, and walk out without explaining where you're going, I will hit you so hard your rock like skin will shatter."

Hugging her back, I say, "Yes ma'am, and I love you too. Can we go inside now?"

Dragging me into Catherine's apartment by the wrist, Jenny notices the still wet blood and asks, "What the hell did you get into this time? It's not like you've been gone very long."

Knowing she can read my thoughts, I say a partial truth, "Nothing too bad, just had a little talk with the nice officer from earlier."

Catherine hears what I said, and chuckles then says, "Good, that little prick was kind of pushy."

Shocked by Catherine's bluntness, Jenny and I stopped dead in our tracks to ponder how something like that came out of this sweet old ladies mouth. We know our reaction got her attention, because she says, "Well, he was." This made all three of us laugh for a moment.

While Jenny sat back down I went to the kitchen to wash the blood from my hands. On my way back to the couch I say, "I did get some good intel from the nice officer before he had to leave."

Jenny looks up from the book she had just started flipping through, and say, "Oh really, do tell."

Sitting down next to Jenny, I say, "For one thing, I now know that two of the twelve are the head of the jail and a police captain. Also he mentioned that they all hang out at the Renaissance festival dressed as knights. Our little Officer Friendly works for them, and his real name is Steven Hatch. He tried to give me some sad story about them threatening his family if he didn't do as they said, but my keen detective skills knew it was a lie. Well that, and he was wearing a pendant that matches the one on the daggers."

Awestruck, Jenny gasps and says, "So now we have to worry about not just some random weirdos but the cops as well. This is great, we are so screwed."

Catherine sips her drink, clears her throat and says, "Not necessarily, this place is safe, and nobody can get in without my say so. You two are welcome to stay as long as you need."

Jenny and I looked at each other for a second and realize it wouldn't work, so I say, "That's awfully nice of you, but I think we need to be out there to deal with the problem head on. I don't think they will expect us to take the fight to them, and that's what I'm going to do."

Catherine shook her head, showing she understands and says, "That's fine and dandy, but if you need a place to sleep you have one."

Jenny gives her a smile and says, "Thank you so much. It really means a lot."

As we get up to leave i remember all the books in the attic and say, "Would it be okay to leave some books, scrolls and stuff here, while we are out and about so nobody takes them? They are all really old, and I would hate for someone to take them."

Catherine gets up to walk us to the door and say, "Of course, you can just put them over near the book shelf."

We thank her again and head up to the attic, gathering up all of the things we salvaged from my apartment. After dropping off the bundles to Catherine's, I sense Jenny's need to go back to her house to make sure Sarah is okay. With nothing more than a nob, she knows I'm ready to go.

As she drives, I tuck the shotgun and two of the daggers under the seat. With a little tape I find in the glove box, I secure one of the daggers to my forearm. Pulling my sleeve down, I look over my arm to see how well it's hidden. Passing the final dagger to Jenny, who tucks it into her inside jacket pocket, for easy access.

We sensed each others nerves as we turned onto Jenny's street. I'm learning that there are certain things I can keep from her, but strong emotions are not one of them. I reach over to grip her hand, letting her know that I'm here for her. As she returned the gesture, I could feel her energy flow into mine.

Releasing her tight grip on my hand, she parks the rumbling beast on the street two houses down from her own. I look towards her to see if she is ready to go, as our eyes met, she is startled. Jenny leans closer and says, "Your eyes, they're glowing."

I flip down the visor and look in the vanity mirror, and sure enough, they were glowing. As I looked closer, it was less of a glow and more of a sparking. It wasn't effecting my vision, that I could tell at first. It wasn't until I really stared at my reflection, that I could see the obsidian like skin forming under my face. Turning, I decided to try and focus on Jenny. The electricity flowing through her veins, her essence, her being, was drawing me in. Touching her arm, I notice that our hidden forms merge. We are as one. There was no boundary between what was her, and where I began. Is this what we had read about, the joining and being unstoppable? Was this what all those people throughout the years have been trying to prevent?

Jenny pulled her arm away and snapped her fingers in front of my face, causing me to lose focus. Touching my cheek with her hand gently she says, "Are you okay, babe? What's wrong, you look spooked?"

Giving her a grin, I say, "Not spooked at all. It's.... it's just that I could see. I mean truly see, what we look like."

Confused Jenny says, "When you say what we look like, do you mean our evolution, or whatever they call it?"

Excited, I say, "Yes, and when I touched you, I could see us blend together as one." Jenny a little freaked out, gets out of the car without waiting for me. I take off my seatbelt and quickly follow her, gently grabbing her arm as she is walking, trying to get her to stop.

Turning quickly, she pulled her arm away from me, saying in an irritated tone, "What, what could be so important that you need to stop me from checking on my friend?"

As apologetic as I can muster, I say, "Sorry, I didn't mean to grab you, I just wanted to get you to wait for a second before rushing in there."

Now seeming more agitated, standing with her arms crossed tapping her foot, Jenny says, "I know you don't like her, but Sarah is my friend and is probably worried sick after what happened last night. So for you to say I'm going off half-cocked, is bullshit."

Defensive I say, "I never said you were half-cocked, and I never said we shouldn't come here and make sure she's okay. What I was trying to say is that we need to be careful, since you know there is currently at least a dozen people gunning for us."

Reaching for Jenny with open arms, attempting to hug her, she steps forward into my embrace and says, "Sorry, I know I can be crazy at times. It's just..." As she was talking I hear movement between a few cars just ahead of us. Not wanting to startle Jenny, I let her continue, "It's just, I want you guys to get along and it sucks that you don't. Do you still love me?"

Pulling her in closer, I scan the area trying to focus and use my new gift, I say, "Of course I still love you. If I wouldn't let a giant soul sucking Sumerian lesser god get in the way of that, do you think I would let your bitch of a roommate stop me?"

Jenny smacked my chest as soon as the comment came out of my mouth. Her hitting me, sparked my eyes into full gear. My focus narrows and I see the outline of two average sized males, ducked down between the cars and one more on the other side of the line of bushes near Jenny's walkway.

Doing my best to act normal, I kiss her on her forehead and lean down, acting like I'm kissing her neck, I whisper, "There's three people hiding, not far from us. Act normal and we can take them before they get us."

In my head, I hear her voice say "Where at?"

Telepathically, I say "There's two ducked down about fifteen feet away and one on other side of your bushes."

So we don't raise any suspicion, verbally in a joking tone I say, "Okay babe, let's go inside so I can apologize to your friend for freaking her out."

'Releasing our embrace, as Jenny backs up, I see she is now palming the dagger that was inside her coat. I give her a smile, as almost saying that's my girl, and slide my arm into the cuff of my sleeve to loosen the tape of the dagger I have tucked away. Knowing we were as ready as we will ever be, we head towards the walkway in front of Jenny's house. I take the left side nearest the street to prevent the possibility of Jenny getting hit with whatever they decided to bring.

The two on our left stay put as we pass, not sure if they are waiting to jump us from behind. We keep our cool as we get to the walkway and on up the concrete strip, still nothing. Jenny gets her keys out of her pocket as we make it to the front porch. I feel something isn't right and she can tell.

In order to stall going inside, Jenny says, "Hey babe, would you do me a favor? I left my phone in car, can you grab it for me before we get in and comfortable, please? You know I'll forget it if we don't get it now."

Knowing what she's trying to do, I say, "Sure, where'd you leave it?"

Playing coy she says, "Ummm, I think it's in the center console, if not there's a chance it fell under your seat."

Taking her keys, I start down the stairs and say, "Cool, be right back." I walk fast looking down as i flip through the keys to find the right one. I can see out of the corner of my eye as I pass the spot where the two were hiding that they weren't there.

I wait to look around until I get in the car and start feeling around for the phone. Once focused I see that all three were together now behind the bush and only about eight feet from Jenny's current location.

Gripping the stock of the shotgun, I yell out to Jenny, "Got it!" Sliding it into my jacket, I get out of the car and lock the door. Jogging back up to the front door I toss the keys to Jenny and telepathically let her know where they are hiding and to get inside.

Not wasting another moment waiting on them to make their move, I dive over the bushes and roll to my feet ready to swing the ax at the first one to move. Frightened one of the men pulled a gun and fired. The round hit me in the midsection, not even leaving a scratch. Swinging the ax as hard as I can, I connect with the mans pistol, knocking it from his hand and severing his finger.

As the street light clicks on, the shadow the men are in vanishes. Now I can clearly see that they are wearing uniforms, not the same as the officer from earlier. The light bounces off of one mans polished metal collar emblem that has the letters C O., Corrections Officers, they were sending everyone after us, but why?

The other two men jump to their feet ready to attack as the third lay bleeding, holding his hand clenched to his chest. I toss the shotgun to Jenny to provide cover in case others try something while I deal with these two. Reaching into my sleeve I pull out the hidden dagger, just as the man to my right lunges at me with a knife of his own. Pivoting to my left, I dodge this thrust. Immediately, the man on my left swings a baton, connecting with my shoulder. Faking like it hurt, I drop to one knee. With the dagger in my left hand, I reach and slice the attacker on the left behind the knee. Quickly I drive the blade clear to the hilt into the right attackers lead foot.

Now all three men, lay bleeding on the grass. Wanting to keep an eye on them I say to Jenny, "Grab Sarah, and meet me at the car. Hurry because we don't know how many more are on the way!"

She turns, opening the door and heads inside, leaving the door open. While she's getting Sarah, I rip the dagger from the guys foot. Pushing him onto his back with my foot, I knell on his chest. The man takes a blind swing at my head. I catch his hand and slam it to the ground. Taking the dagger I drag the blade under his chin to let him know that I mean business, and to not try it again.

Once he stops squirming, I pull the dagger blade away from his throat. As I do, I see a chain sticking out from under the edge of his shirt collar. With the tip of the blade I catch the chain, and just as I thought it reveals a cross pendant matching the nice officers from earlier. With no questions left to ask of who sent them, i rip the chain free and punch him as hard as I can, knocking him out.

With one down, there was only two to go. I see the man with the bleeding knee starting to crawl away. Taking two steps, I leap, landing square in the middle of his back. This causes him to collapse to the ground, letting out a loud cry of pain. Yanking his collar back, I find yet another matching chain. Breaking it free with one swift motion, I climb of of his back and head toward the third and final contestant.

He must have been the brains of the group, because before I had even reached him he had the chain off. He was holding it out to me like it was a gift, that I graciously accepted. Raring my leg back to plant a steel toe boot to the side of his face he says, "They will never stop coming, they never have." Then his eyes went blank and passes out.

I look up, just in time to see Sarah running out the door followed closely by Jenny. At the speed they were moving I can only assume something was after them. My thought was confirmed as Jenny turns, firing the shotgun at a man stepping through the doorway. The shot levels him, sending him falling flat on his back with a fist sized hole in his gut.

Stuffing the pendants in my pants pocket, in a hurry I make my way to the end of the row of bushes. By the time I get to the car, Sarah is climbing in the back seat and Jenny has the key in the ignition. I flip the seat back and climb in just as I hear the engine rev. I slam my door in time for her to drop the Camaro into gear. The tires smoke as Jenny floors the gas pedal. A quick cut of the wheel and we were on our way out of there.

Once we are a little over three blocks away, Jenny slowed down to match the speed limit. Knowing that the cops are involved, we don't need to draw any unwanted attention to ourselves. Things are bad enough without accidentally having a good cop caught in the crossfire.

In the passing light of a street lamp, I catch the glossy, red blood on my hands. While wiping them off on my shirt I notice that my midsection was tacky and wet. Grabbing my phone from my pocket, I use the light from the screen to get a better look at my shirt. I think back, trying to remember when or if I got close enough to get this much blood on me. Upon pulling up my shirt I see the small hole a few inches above my navel. The blood streams from the wound slightly faster than a trickle.

Jenny, so lost in the getaway, hadn't noticed my bleeding. Glancing over to see why I was using my phone, she sees the pool of blood on my lap. Panicked, Jenny slams on the breaks, causing me to drop my phone. Bathed in the light of the street lamps, the blood didn't look real. I felt no pain, no pressure, no different.

Sarah shifted to behind the drivers seat, as I laid my seat back so Jenny could get a better look at the entry wound. With the amount of blood loss, I figure that I should at least feel drained. Jenny digs through the center console and finds a small flashlight that she keeps tucked in there. Usually she uses it for reading addresses for food delivery, but she never thought it would be used to examine a gunshot wound.

Clicking the button on the end of the flashlight, the car illuminates with the bright glow of the five LED bulbs shinning in unison. She barks an order to Sarah, "Hold the light right here! I need both hands to try to stop the bleeding!" Sarah complies without a word. I can only imagine that her silence is a result of shock.

Pushing up her sleeves, Jenny leans in for a closer look. Sitting back upright she takes a only a second before her hand dives to the floorboard between my legs. When she sits up, I see her holding a white rag. Franticly she wipes the blood away from the wound with the rag. The rags soaked through more and more with every swipe. As she applies pressure, her hand slips off the blood caked rag coming to rest on the exposed black flesh. Upon contact with the bullet hole, the bleeding stopped. Sparks slowly formed, giving off blue flashes growing brighter the longer she holds the wound.

As my body was consumed by her electric touch, I feel Jenny's life force merging with mine. It was powering me to heal. The tingle that I first felt grew to a burn. I can feel the hole closing from her touch. Tilting my head forward, I see Jenny's eyes engulfed in the blue flame. While trying to get at look at my stomach, I'm astonished when I notice her hands absorbing my blood. As the sparks fly, the blood flow reverses causing the pools to drain rapidly. It was either her absorbing my blood or our life forces merging that was causing her trance-like state. One thing for sure it was really getting to our passenger. Sarah's breathing became erratic, and from the way the light was bouncing around, I knew her tremors were worsening. If she didn't calm down soon Sarah would hyperventilate and pass out.

As the wound closed, I received a burst of power that sends a shockwave through the car. The blast radiates outward rendering both Jenny and Sarah unconscious upon impact. The side windows buckle and shatter as well as spider webbing the windshield and back glass.

Having no choice, I open my door and climb out with the seat still leaned back. I take hold of Jenny's arms and pull her limp body to the passenger seat. Not wasting time with buckling her in, I slam the door and hurry to the drivers side. The crunch of glass resonates with each rushed step. Swinging the door open, sends the remaining door glass flying. In one fluid motion, I jump in the seat and close the door. Shifting hard into drive with the gas to the floor, the Camaro lurches forward like a scalded dog.

Lost in a city where I lived, no destination to speak of, I aimlessly drive the empty streets. My concern grows with each passing breath. Neither of them has moved, no groans, no twitches that I've noticed. There had to be somewhere to go, someone who can help. They had to be watching the bookstore as well as the apartment building.

I've never known or thought to ask where Mother or Sebastian lived at. The way the windows looked, I knew it was only time before I would be pulled over and have to explain why I have a messed up windshield and there were two unresponsive girls in the car. Not to mention the blood or my black rock-like skin.

The only place I think of that might be deserted enough to hide out is only a few minutes away. That is if I can figure out how to get there from where ever the hell we are. It takes me a few wrong turns to get on track and we arrive in the run down area known as the west bottoms. The west bottoms is what remains of the warehouse district and what use to be the slaughterhouse area for the livestock auctions. The only thing here now are vacant buildings, haunted houses and most likely meth labs. This area was great if you wanted to disappear for a while or get a nights sleep without worrying about getting rolled or hassled by the cops. There were too many alleyways and corridors that someone could hide in, if you were brave enough to try.

Carefully, I check the area. With not a living soul in sight, I return to the car. I grab a few boxes and old bags of trash and toss them in front of the car to disguise our arrival as just another abandoned junker. Repeating the process on the rear of the car, I feel it should be good enough for one night at least. Getting my arms under Jenny, I pull her close as I attempt to get her out of the car without dropping her or smacking her face on the door frame.

Once she was clear of the door frame, I stand up and turn setting her on the edge of an old loading dock. The thing doesn't look like it's been used in close to three decades. Sarah was going to be the difficult one with her in the back seat. Luckily I wasn't too concerned with her being banged around as I pull her out of the car. I lay her next to Jenny, causing the wood of the dock to creak and settle under the weight. I get ready to close the door when I remember to grab my phone and the flashlight. Something tells me that there wasn't going to be electricity, much less proper lighting.

Testing a few doors to see if they were locked, and looking in a few dirt covered windows, I found my way in. With one swing of my trusty ax, the chain was cleaved in two. It took a few solid tugs to get the rust to break free allowing the door to open. Pulling the flashlight out of my pocket, clicking the button as I got it chest level. The room was flooded with light, showing me exactly how much dust I managed to kick up when the breeze made its way inside.

It only takes me a moment to realize that this place was an old slaughterhouse, from the meat hooks and stainless steel prepping tables. I do my best clearing the layers of filth off of two of the tables with handfuls of wadded up butcher paper that I find on the floor.

One at a time I carry them in. Laying each on a separate table. I take off my hoodie and place it under Jenny's head, and a ball of paper under Sarah's.

I check for a pulse on Jenny and feel a faint but present beating, when I hear a moan come from Sarah's table. Rushing to her side, I tell her to stay down until I've had a chance to check her for injuries. She does as asked, too groggy to really fight it if she wanted to.

Not knowing a thing about how to treat any injury that I find, the thought crosses my mind to try to use my new gift. I focus my eyes, allowing the gift to take over. In a scanning motion, I slowly follow the contours of Sarah's body not seeing anything that I can tell is wrong. I turn my attention to Jenny. The energy that I noticed in her early was drasticly lower now. With my touch, I see the energy grow. At risk of draining myself, I grab hold of her arm with both hands.

I hear Sarah move behind me and turn to look. As my glance leaves Jenny, with my eyes still focused I see the faint outline of several humanoid figures standing just out of the room. They appear to be watching me. Losing focus from the surprise, my normal vision returns. The images vanish as if they were never there.

Keeping one hand on Jenny to transfer some of her energy back, I look over my shoulder at Sarah. She's sitting upright with her feet hanging off of the table. She uses one hand to rub her head and the other to hold the table for balance. She may be a little off for a bit, and that is fine with me because I have no idea how I'm going to explain any of this without Jenny.

I snap my fingers a few times to get Sarah's attention and say "I know things are rather confusing right now, and we will get to that in a minute. Jenny needs our help, so you need to snap out of it and get over here."

Slowly she slides off the table and comes to the side of where Jenny is laid out. Shaking her head to try to help wake up she says, "What do you want me to do?"

Trying to buy some time to figure out what those figures were I say, "Here take her wrist and keep track of her pulse. If it starts to slow down, let me know. I'm going to see if there's anything I can use to keep you two warm."

I didn't wait for her reply before I walked to the doorway. Refocusing, I see the figures never left. They were surrounding us on all sides. They bowed their heads as I approached them individually as if they were afraid. Looming back at Jenny, I see them surrounding her and they simultaneously reach for her. A stream of energy left their collective bodies and passed directly into her. I can see her life force rapidly increase, returning her to the way she was before. As Jenny came to they backed away, fading gradually till they were no where to be found.

Rather than freak the two of them out more, I conclude keeping what I just witnessed to myself for the time being. My main focus at the moment is to make sure the girls are fine. I go to their side, and say, "Are you okay, how are you two feeling? Jenny? Sarah?"

Sarah still using the table to help balance says, "Other than a little wobbly, I'm fine. I would like to know what the hell was all that back at the house, and that shit in the car. I mean, I knew you were a freak, but did you infect Jenny too or something?"

Before I had a chance to snap back at the freak comment, Jenny says, "First off, knock off the freak talk, he's more special than you know. Second, no he didn't 'infect' me, I've always been like this. Just around him it's amplified. So I guess we are just a pair of freaks to you. Take it or leave it, but us freaks just saved your life."

Sarah shakes her head and hops up on the table next to Jenny and says, "Whatever, sorry about the freak thing. You know I can't stay mad at you, but you still need to explain why you needed to save me in the first place."

Stepping in front of them both I say, "Well that's pretty much my fault. I'm not really sure how to explain this to you but I will give it a shot. Okay here we go. I am some kind of demigod. Short version of it is, my parents were the high gods of ancient Sumaira. People have been keeping Jenny and I apart for thousands of years because together we are too powerful for them to control. We live, we die over, and over and this is the first time we have ever been this close. Now I'm evolving to my god form or something and her powers are growing. The people wanting to kill you were after us because they want something we have. Hey babe, how was that?"

Jenny looks up at me and say, "Yeah, that sums it up. Oh, you forgot that there's more gifted out there and we have others we work with on this."

I feeling a little released getting out there for her to know say, "And I had to kill a giant lesser god that wanted to steal our abilities the other day. That's how the two of us met. He was trying to kidnap Jenny."

Sarah holds up her hands like she was giving up and says, "You guys are messing with me, right? You can't be serious, gods, magic assassins. None of that stuff is real."

Jenny points at me and says, "I guess we should show her. Take off your shirt."

Confused about her request I say, "Why do I need to strip for your friend?"

Jenny, looking annoyed says, "Your skin, dumbass. Show her the skin on your chest."

Feeling like an idiot, I say, "Oh yeah, I knew what you meant." I take off my shirt, showing the onyx skin covering my torso and arms. Slowly spinning in a circle to reveal exactly how much of my body was like this. Jenny hops off the table and steps beside me. Once I face Sarah, Jenny places her hand on my chest and drags it across from right to left. The sparks trail her fingers causing the black skin to glow the bright electric blue.

A gasp came from Sarah as the new reality sets in. I put my shirt on and reach my left arm towards her and say, "You can touch it if you want."

"No I'm fine, but you said there are others like you out there." Sarah says with a worried expression.

Jenny moved closer to comfort her friend and says, "Well not exactly like us. From what we are told we are unique in what we can do. We don't know too much about others because we are just finding stuff out ourselves. If it wasn't for this lady we call Mother, we wouldn't know anything at all."

Leaning on Jenny, Sarah seems confused and accepting of what she just saw. After a moment Sarah asks, "Does anyone else know, you know, what you are?"

Without thinking I blurt out, "Fred does. He might have known before we did since he worked for the god I killed, but this guy Sebastian and I killed his entire crew and beat the shit out of him. Don't worry, were all good now. He's part of the team." From the look on her face, I knew I said more than I should have. I could feel Jenny's eyes burning into me as well.

Jenny hugs Sarah and says, "You will have to get use to it. Genius here, doesn't think things through before he says things. He may not be the smartest one but he's good to me and won't let anything happen to me either."

Sarah smiles slightly and says, "Well, I guess he did take on a god for you."

Feeling like I'm intruding on their girl time I say, "You girls relax for a bit and I'm going to secure the door and then check the building out to see if there's a better place to hunker down in here for the night."

Jenny grabs the flashlight off of the table and says, "You get the door, and we'll go with you to check it out. No need for you to have to double back for us if you find something. Knowing you, you'll get lost or distracted and leave us back here bored."

If there was anything I've learned it's that there is no use in arguing. I head to the door to see what can be done to get it to stay closed. I see the chain that I busted off laying on the ground. Picking it up, I fish it through the hole. Now to find a way to connect it. Looking over the room, I see a meat hook hanging near by. Grabbing the hook, I pry both ends of the chain over the pointed tip. With all of my strength, gripping the metal firmly, I bend the hook. Convinced it should hold, I admire my handy work. Turning to rejoin the girls, I notice the look of astonishment on both of their faces. Not wanting to explain it, since I'm not even sure how I did it, I say, "Okay, lets do this,'' and walk out of the room picking up my shotgun on the way out the door.

In the hallway, I trade Jenny the shotgun for the flash light. Leading the way so I'm the first one to face any awaiting danger. Sarah follows behind me, with Jenny bringing up the rear with the shotgun. Room after filthy room, we check with nothing to see except more dirt covered stainless steel equipment. Most of the building looks like its been picked over by scrappers years ago. It isn't until we reach the third floor that we find the what we were in search of, the bosses office.

A light from an adjacent building shines partially into the room, providing just enough light to see the layout. The plush office gave the appearance that the former owners had every intention of coming back. The furniture lay under covers, preventing them from being damaged by the elements. I peal back the covers slowly so I don't stir up more dust and look over our find. Judging by the quality of leather that was used, this had to have cost someone a pretty penny, and it's hard to believe that it was just left like it was.

I close and lock the office door. It seems to be solid wood, which will provide some peace of mind as our first level of protection if anyone comes looking around. I pull one of the heavy leather chair over to the door to help brace it closed. Looking over to the see where Jenny and Sarah were, since they were being so quiet. I find them cuddled up on the couch together on the couch sleeping. Picking up the shotgun from the floor by the couch, I go back to the chair I placed against the door. It didn't take me long to get comfortable and feel sleep coming on fast.

I wake with a jolt at the sound of a near by door being kicked in. Startled, it takes me a moment to realize that I wasn't me. I was in the same office as I went to sleep in, but everything is different. There was no dust, no layer of film on the windows. Everything was clean and new. I catch a glimpse of my reflection in a mirror that stands in the corner of the office. I appear to be in a balding, middle-aged man. The clothes weren't from recent fashion but were form fitting and good quality.

The sound of another door being kicked in, rings down the hallway. This one was closer than the last. I feel the panic radiate through this man as he stood frozen in fear. As if by the flip of a switch, complete clarity took over the man. He hits a button under his desk. The echo of locks slamming into place on the office door, and a panel on the wall quietly pops open revealing a hidden room just behind his desk.

The man enters the dark hidden room without haste. He pulls the door closed quickly. I feel his hand running across the wall in search of something, then his fingers find it.

The dim light gives off just enough light to see in the small area. As the shadows bounce from wall to wall, I notice that this was more than just a tiny panic room. Gradually a few more lights come to life, showing the long corridor of this hidden area. Before he ventures down the corridor, the man slides a crossbar between the door and wall. I feel his sense of security rise as he starts his journey through his barely lit hiding spot.

As the man made his way through, I can't help but notice the walls. They are cluttered with various trinkets. Most of them had crosses, others had unrecognizable symbols and glyphs. If they were locked up in they place, I knew they had to be special in some way or another.

The man stops as the voices on the other side of the wall go from a low mumble to a more audible volume. The concussion of another door splintering rattles the wall. The high pitched screams of what appears to be multiple women, pierce the air. They are quickly followed by gargling choking sounds.

A mans voice comes through the wall saying, "Where is it? He's got to have it somewhere. You two, go check the office across the hall!"

Another male voice answers saying, "You got it." Only a few seconds pass when the second man says, "I think our rat, gave us bad info. The guys not here. Hell the door wasn't even locked."

Heavy footsteps fall as the first man moves toward the office where we had escaped from. The first man says, "I'm going to gut that snitch. We have to find something to take back to the Twelve, or it's our heads that will roll. Check everywhere, under the carpet, on or behind the shelves, behind mirrors and pictures. He has to have a safe hiding somewhere."

The sounds of things being thrown around fills my ears. The man I'm in slowly makes his way further down the corridor away from the ruckus. Reaching the far wall he stops. He turns to the right. There in front of us is a large mirror. The frame was covered in ornamental gold designs on a blackened leather. The mirror didn't appear to be glass, but a highly polished silvery metal.

Bowing his head, I hear the man whisper words in a language that I can't understand. He raises his head, looking straight into his reflections eyes and says "My prince, I've waited the day that you would choose to enter me as a vessel. This day was foretold by the one they call Mother when she took my great grandfather Sebastian as her protector. I have used my position to acquire you these relics. I hope you are able to use them. My time is over on this plain and it was an honor to have served you."

Without warning he drug a knife across his throat. As the blood flowed out our connection grew weaker until it was gone.

Opening my eyes, there in front of me stands Jenny and Sarah. Mouths wide open, eyes fixed on my neck. The expressions they have was a combination of horror and awe. Sitting up I say, "What's going on? You guys are kinda freaking me out staring at me like that."

Jenny moved forward and squatted down in front of me and asks, "Were you, you know, inside someone else?"

"Yeah, why do you ask? Did something happen while I was out?" I ask in a groggy confused voice.

I could see the concern in her eyes when Jenny says, "We woke up just a little bit ago and when we checked on you, well you wouldn't respond. When we got closer, you weren't breathing. Then from out of nowhere, you sit straight up, eyes wide open glowing bright blue. Not even a second later, your throat lit up like a neon sign. It was bright enough that we had to look away."

Somewhat amazed I say, "I've never been around anyone when I've traveled before. Kinda cool if you ask me."

Annoyed with my response, Jenny says, "Yeah, cool. Glad you're not dead."

With her frustration clear, apologetically I say, "Sorry babe, I'm still getting use to someone being around. I'm not going to say it won't happen again, because there's no way to know. If it means anything to you, I think we were supposed to find this place." The two of them stared at me more confused than before when I got up and went to the desk.

My fingers fish around under the edge of the desk. Finding the slight indentation on the underside next to the drawer, I push. The office door shutters when the locks engage. Behind me a burst of stale air hits me, escaping from the hidden room. Motioning for them to join me, I say, "Grab the flashlight and the shotgun and come here."

With hesitation in her voice Sarah says, "How did he know that was there, how is any of this even happening?"

Jenny more use to me doing things impulsive, is already gathering up the shotgun and handing Sarah the flashlight saying, "He does weird stuff all the time. I find it's easier to just go with it."

They follow me into the room. The unsteady hand of Sarah was making the light from the flashlight bounce off of every surface. Once they are inside the room, I close the door and flip the light switch several times, no result. The bulbs had probably burned out decades ago.

The bouncing light from the way Sarah held it was starting to get to me. I take the flashlight and set it on a ledge that's just about shoulder lever while I think. The flashlight rolls as it settles. The stream of light bounces from polished surface to polished surface on the relics creating plenty of light to see.

The amount of dust was minimal compared to the rest of the building. I'm not sure if it was the sealed door, lack of vents, or if there was another reason, but it was welcome. Lately, I've managed my fair share digging through dirt and grime between the attic hideout and Jacqueline's backroom.

I get my phone out to catalog the relics by taking pictures of each item in the corridor. I have a feeling Mother is going to want to know what was found. I tell Sarah to wipe the dust off in front of each item that i snap a picture of so we can keep track. There were shields, instruments made of various materials, goblets, weapons, a few things that I couldn't name. A few items seemed out of place. They looked more like junk, than some important relic. Among the odd things is the jawbone of a large animal like a horse, a broken spear tip, a bundle of hair, a broken antler with what I assume is blood on it, a large jar of salt and an apple that someone had already started eating. The apple was probably just the guys snack that was left behind. Seriously, what good would an old apple be.

As we continue the cataloging, I had forgotten the ending of my hitchhiking vision. The fresh air that entered the room from our invasion of the corridor, has released an odor of must and decay. I tried to push passed the stench until my foot hit something blocking my route. Looking down, I find the source of the aroma. I've seen my share of dead recently, but none that I've inhabited just a sort time ago. Even though he had just talked to me an hour ago, seeing his rapidly decaying corpse laying there sends a chill up my spine. Being stuck in this sealed room, must have preserved his body. Well, it would have if I wouldn't have popped the cork and let time catch up to him.

I stand frozen, watching nature take its course faster than I knew was possible. Jenny nudges me to try to get a look at whatever has my attention. Turning quickly, I say, "You two don't need to see this."

Jenny, showing no fear, looks passed my left arm. Her eyes widen when she notices what had caught my attention and says, "What...who..how is that possible?"

Pushing them back away from the body, I say, "I don't know, I'm not a scientist. What I do know is that I want that door open, and I think we've gotten enough pictures for now."

Sarah both curious and frightened by what Jenny and I saw, was trying to catch a glimpse as we made our way back to the door. "What's back there, why can't I see?" She says.

Jenny knowing her friend, says "Trust me, you don't want to see. It's haunting."

Sarah trusts Jenny's judgment, says, "If you say so, but could someone at least tell me what it was?"

Tired of beating around the bush, I say, "It's a rotting corpse, a thirty plus year old corpse that didn't start to fall apart until the fresh air hit it. Are you happy now?"

Jenny shocked by my abruptness and attitude towards Sarah, elbows me in the sternum. Her loss of control sent a shockwave through my body, causing me to slide backwards a few feet. I probably would have gone further if I hadn't have caught myself on the shelving.

Surprised by the effect of her strike, she rushes over to me. As she reaches for me, I stick out my hands to stop her and say, "Woo now, Bruce Lee."

Jenny apologetic says, "I'm sorry babe, I still don't know how to control this thing."

Rubbing my chest where she connected I say, "I'll be fine, you just need to give me a minute. Maybe Mother can help you learn control. First let's get out of this place. It's starting to feel a little cramped."

I grab the flashlight off of the shelf as I walk to the door. Cranking the locking handle, I feel it start to turn. The vibration of my phone in my pocket stops me. Checking it, I see a message from Mother. It was short and to the point.

"Get to the store"

I look to my companions and say, "Well, looks like we might be getting some answers. We've been summoned." I show Jenny the text, and one solid twist the lock opens releasing the door.

Back in the office, I secure the door to the hidden room. We put the covers back on the furniture, in hopes of making it look undisturbed. I open the office door slowly to check out in the hallway first before just barging out blindly and hear movement. Focusing my sight, I try to see if I can see what was making the sounds. There in front of me is one of the shadow figures. It was directing me to follow it. After the display earlier with Jenny I feel they are here to help us. Waving for Jenny and Sarah to follow me and to be quiet, Sarah removes her shoes. Having a hard sole, they would surely draw attention.

The dark silhouette ushered the three of us slowly from hallway to hallway. We went through offices to avoid certain areas, stopped and told to duck down in others. Instead of heading down stairs to the car, it lead us up. I'm not known for blindly following anyone, but something told me that it is the best and only option we have with the amount of movement we are hearing. The footsteps grew further away, the further we went up in the building.

Reaching the roof, through a hatch we were directed to in a storage closet, the crisp early morning air let us know we are almost safe. The concrete roof allows us to move more quickly behind the figure. Reaching the edge of the roof, for a moment seemed to indicate the end of the road. The figure pointed to an adjacent rooftop just a few feet away.

Jumping the gap won't be a problem for me, but not sure how the girls are going to feel about it. I gave a nod to the figure as thanks. With one last look at the way we came, I take a few quick step and leap. Clearing the gap with no problem. I motion for Jenny to follow me when the stairwell door flings open, just twenty feet from them.

Jenny tosses my the shotgun as her and Sarah run towards the edge of the roof. I catch it by the grip with my left hand. As the girls land, I fire off one shot as four men clear the doorway. The shot hits the frame of the door, making the men drop and take cover. This buys us a few valuable seconds to make a break for a way down.

The men don't follow, allowing the three of us to clear two more roofs as fast as we can move our legs. Them not following, gave me an uneasy feeling. Either they wanted us to get away, knew that we would run out of room to run and they would be waiting. My heavy steps proved it was neither one, as the roof began to crumble. We split up staying several feet apart to try and spread the weight over the area instead of all together.

We slowed our pace to a fast walk, taking careful steps on this unsure material. I find my footing on a seemingly solid cross beam, when the roof gives way under Sarah's feet. Diving, I catch her hand before it disappears completely into the darkness. Throwing caution to the wind, Jenny darts to my side. I feel the roof dip under our combined weight and instruct her to stay on the beam where my feet lay. She grabs my ankles tightly, transferring her energy into me. The added power gives me enough strength to pull Sarah free from the collapsed depths.

Following the exposed beams, slowly we work our way to the to the end of the line. I look over the edge with dread, not knowing what I might find. The six story drop was less than inviting.

The nearest building was at least thirty feet away on the other side of the street. The fire escape on our building was on the other side of the massive cavern that I just pulled Sarah out of and no safe way around it.

To our right, I can make out the river. Jenny notices me eyeing the waterfront, and her fear sets in. Climbing onto the small ledge, I give Jenny a smile and say, "Got to risk it, for the biscuit." Blowing her a kiss, I take off running as fast as I can and jump.

Eyes closed, I was afraid to see where or on what I might land on. The sudden impact caught me off guard. I open my eyes with just enough time to catch myself from falling off a smaller structure only two floors below where I had jumped from. Getting myself to my feet, I realize that the building was blocking the view of where I had landed. Before I can yell for them not to follow, I see Jenny falling towards me. I use my body to cushion her landing, catching her before she hit the roof hard. I wasn't able to regain footing when Sarah struck me in the back hard, driving me into the ground.

Shaking off the surprise dropkick, I walk slowly around the edge looking for a way down. I see a dumpster full of trash bags on the ground on the north side of the building. It appears to be the fastest way down to the ground but I feel I should check with the others first, I say, "Hey there's a full dumpster down here, anyone feel like jumping again?"

Jenny peeks over the edge to see what I'm talking about. Without another word, she shoves me off. I fall clumsily off the building and land dead center on a pile of bags. They were full of what seemed like paper old food, probably from one of the recent street festival. It was enough to stop me from breaking anything. I climb out of the dumpster and wave for Jenny to jump. She steps off the roof and laid back, landing more gracefully than I could ever try to.

I help her out, and wave for Sarah. She hesitates for just a minute, but when I see her look behind her quickly, I knew there was something wrong. Stepping off the roof, she fell like a rock. Straight legging her fall into the dumpster. Sarah wasted no time getting out, still looking up. We needed to get out of here before they close in on us and leave us no where to run.

I figure the car was compromised, since the ones searching for us knew what building we were in. As we sneak from building to building, shadow to shadow through the west bottoms, the urge to ask what Sarah saw that made her jump the way she did keeps nagging me. I better leave it alone for now. We have more important things to deal with.

We make it out of the maze of alleyways and across the street from a gas station. I spot a cab getting gas at the pump. His duty light is off, but usually if the pay is enough they will still get you where they need to go. I send the girls up to him to ask if they can get a ride from here, it looks promising.

Getting the wave to hurry from Jenny, I run over to join them. Seeing me, the cab driver tries to refuse. Well, that is until I hand him my last bit of cash. It was probably only a hundred dollars, but it did the trick. Ducking down in the back between the girls. We were off to the book store. The cab went east up the 12th street bridge, giving us an excellent view of exactly how many cops were searching the bottoms.

We have the cab driver drop us off at the coffee shop a block from the book store. He doesn't look like he cares who we are, but you never can tell. He would probably dime out his own family if the right price is reached. Sarah doesn't have a clue where we were heading, so I lead the way to the rear door in the alley. A few soft taps, and the door opens.

Standing in the doorway is Fred. He's wearing a red flowered kimono, that I hope he borrowed from Jacqueline. With the way he was grinning, I wouldn't be surprised if it was his. The look on Sarah's face is priceless. The wonderful mix of unapproving disgust and shame makes me let out a chuckle. I shake his hand as I come inside, accepting the odd as the new normal with our group. Jenny pushes Sarah up the stairs and into the back door of the store. Once inside, Jenny closes and locks the door behind her.

Making our way down the back hallway, I say, "How's it going Fred? I see you made yourself at home."

Looking over his shoulder, he says, "Well, I didn't exactly have time to get more clothes before everything went to shit. My clothes if you must know are drying, and it was either this or run around naked."

Jenny from the back says, "Don't listen to him Fred, the color really brings out your eyes. Besides Jacob's already destroyed like three sets of clothes, and one of them was Karl's."

Sarah says, "Hey, I thought that shirt looked familiar."

Trying to defend myself, I say, "I didn't intend to get shot, and who was it that launched me out of an attic window? Oh yeah that was you."

Fred stops and turns to face me, and asks, "When you say shot, you're talking about with a gun right?"

Shaking my head yes, I say, "Yep, right in the gut."

A little confused, Fred asks, "And that launched you out of the attic window, how high up were you?"

Seeing where he got lost at, I say, "No, I got shot by a cop. She used her gift to launch me out a window. It was the attic of the apartments, so I guess around five or six stories."

Jenny chimes in saying, "I still say both of those were his fault."

Fred and I nodded and in unison say, "She's probably right."

Fred turns and heads towards the backroom, I pat him on the back and we follow. Nervous of how to explain everything that's happened to everyone, I try to get things right in my head. The smell of cleaning solution overpower my senses, bringing back the recent slaughter that took place here. I knew it had to be horrible for Fred as well. He's had a hell of a few weeks, and he's become a part of the team. With that in mind, I make a mental note not to torment him and bring up any of the history.

Entering the backroom, I see Mother and Jacqueline sitting at the table, while Sebastian thumbs through the newspaper. The three of them stop what they are doing as Sarah enters. They almost look more shocked than her. Jenny steps in the room and heads straight for Mother.

She gives Mother a hug and before she can give one to Jacqueline Mother says, "Jacob, don't be rude. Introduce your guest." Her tone let me know she wasn't pleased, and she saw Sarah as more of an intruder than guest.

Jenny spoke up sensing Mother's disapproval, saying, "Sorry, everyone. This is my roommate Sarah." Pointing to each person as she named them off, "This is Mother, Jacqueline, Sebastian over in the corner and you know Fred."

Sarah awkwardly waves at everyone and say, "Hi"

Stepping up I say, "Funny story, the people that were after me, went to her house and were trying to kill her. Probably thought she was Jenny." Jaws drop as I gave my explanation, leaving the room silent. So I say, "Oh yeah, I got something for you guys." Fishing the chains and pendants out of my pocket, I start handing one to each of the four.

Mother looks over the pendant and asks, "Where did you get these, and why do you have so many of them?"

I feel I hit a nerve, so I say, "You remember the guys that were after Sarah, yeah them. Oh and another one that stalking us at the apartment. By the way, Catherine says hello."

Furious Mother says, "You had no business bringing her into this mess."

Defensive I say, "We... we didn't get her involved in anything. She offered us help and shelter, while you failed to tell us some key information." I feel Sebastian's gaze burning into the back of my head. Before he could make a move, I say "You stand down, or do you not remember the last time you sucker punched me in the back."

My temper was flaring, and began to get very hot. Jenny attempts to come to me when she's stopped by Fred. Seeing her being held back, pissed me off more. The temperature of my skin climbed, as my anger grew. Without warning my focus changed on its own, allowing me to see every ones true form. First was Jacqueline, mostly normal with a small spark in her hands. Next, I spun to see Sebastian. He gave off a radiating power. Sarah had nothing special about her in these eyes. Jenny, glowing bright and brilliant as her power flowed in my direction. I can see each and every tattoo on Fred. They pulse a deep black, seeming to drain on his essence. Turning towards Mother, the moment I saw her, my insides boiled and an animalistic nature began to take over.

Mother stands, shouting, "CEASE!"

I drop to one knee, completely drained. I barely had the strength to look up at her before everything went black.

Opening my eyes, I see everyone take a step back away from me. The absolute horror and fear in their eyes. Even Jenny seems afraid of me. With nobody saying anything, I sit up and say, "What's going on, how did I get in this chair?" I smell something burnt, and look down at my clothes. My shirt was still smoldering, and I say, "Who the hell set me on fire?"

"You did babe, are you feeling okay?" Jenny says, her voice trembling.

Confused by why they are acting like this, I say, "Look, I'm sorry I got mad, but I'm pretty sure I would remember setting myself on fire."

Fred comes closer and kneels down next to the chair, and says, "She's telling you the truth, bud. The madder you got, the more flames came out out of you. It was wicked looking."

I start to remember what I saw before I went down. I look directly at Mother. Her eyes go cold, telling me this wasn't the time to bring it up. I give her a slight nod, and she returns it with a partial smile as a thank you.

Looking at my smoldering clothes, I say, "Well, that's not the first new gift that I've experienced in the last two days. It maybe the most dangerous, but I guess we will see what else happens."

Concerned, Mother asks, "What other gifts have you learned you can do, and then we will get to the rest of what happened."

Thinking back, I say, "There's the eye thing. If I focus, I can see others true form and also things that aren't visible to others."

Jenny knowing about the form part, but not the other says, "When you say you can see things that others can't, is that how you knew how to get out of the building?"

"Honestly, I had no clue how to get out. I followed a dark, shadow like creature out of there. He pointed me in the direction to go, when to stop, when to duck down. There is also another part I didn't tell you about how you came to after you healed me." I say, a little afraid to tell her the other part.

Sarah speaks up, saying, "I was wondering about that." Looking at Jenny, she says, "You went from out cold with a low pulse, to strong pulse and back to your old self in a matter of seconds"

I feel the nerves setting in, and before they do, I get it out I say, "You know that shadow thing that lead us out? Well, there were about twenty of them that surrounded you, and passed their energy into you. Sorry, I didn't know what to do. They helped you and that's what counts."

Mother, steps in and says, "Those shadow figures that you saw are called ghasts. They are souls that are trapped here on this plain. They are perfectly harmless, but it's a little unheard of for them to interact like that with the living."

Using the armrest, I push myself to my feet. Stretching, I say, "They not only interacted, they helped big time. I guess the next thing wasn't exactly a new gift, but it was something new that happened with an old gift." Pacing the floor, I say, "During a hitchhiking, I went into someone that has been dead for many decades, but that wasn't the strangest part. The strange part came when he looked into a mirror and talked to me. I don't mean, he talked to himself and it felt like he was talking to me. He straight up knew I was inside him. He mentioned that he knew you." I point at Mother, then to Sebastian and say, "Hell Sebastian, he said he was your great grandson."

Sebastian perked up when I said that. I choose to continue, since nobody was stopping me. I say, "He showed me where he hid a ton of odd relics. How to get in the area, gave a little speech to me, and then he slit his throat. I'm sorry, Sebastian."

Sebastian with his somber demeanor pats me on my shoulder and says, "We never knew what happened to him, now we do. It's good to have closure. I grieved for him long ago and hopefully now he can rest."

Mother in an effort to comfort him, tells Sebastian, "He was a good man, and he said he had a purpose that he couldn't explain."

Feeling uncomfortable with the combination of lack of emotion and the fact that I almost turned into a fireball, I say, "Say, does anyone have a laptop or something. I want to transfer the pictures of the things in that room. Maybe you guys can make heads or tails of them. My relic identification is limited to things from movies on cable."

Fred makes some room on the table by shoving a stack of books to the side. Grabbing his laptop, he sets it up and says, "Here you go, you big flamer. Try not to melt my shit."

Giving Fred a dirty look for the flamer comment, I connect my phone to the laptop and transfer the pictures that I had saved. Once they were ready, I open the gallery and say, "Here goes nothing, stop me when I get to something that you recognize."

The first couple pictures went by without anyone making a sound. I noticed as I clicked that Mother was writing. The list grew longer as each image flipped by. The concern on Mothers face had a slight hint of intrigue. Coming to the last picture, I say, "There were a few more things in there, but you get the idea of what kind of stuff was in hidden away."
Mother motions for me to get out of the chair. Taking over my spot, she starts the pictures over. As they slowly click by she says, "Some of these were thought of as pure myth by most. Somehow Alan, that was his name by the way, got his hands on them. From what you described about the dream, they were meant for you.

Okay, back on topic. We have the apple from the garden of Eden, the spear they used to stab Jesus while he was crucified. That's the horn that brought down the walls of Jericho. That is known as the first blade. It's what is said to have been used by Cain to kill Able. The mirror that he spoke to you through was written about in the tales done by the Grimm brothers. It holds a powerful mage inside, trapped behind the glass. That's how he was able to reach you so long after he passed. We need to get back there and get those things. They need to be locked up some place safe."

Sarah not knowing her place in this twisted group of misfits says, "Seems that they are pretty safe where they are now. Nobody knew they were there for what like 30 or 40 years."

I can't believe I'm about to do it, but I say, "Sarah's right, they stayed hidden for decades, and unless people are inside my head or that room with us they don't know how to get in there. Also that place was crawling with people looking for us. It's not going to be easy to get back in there and haul a bunch of crap out without being noticed."

"I got an idea" Fred says as he's messing with his phone. He has a big grin on his face.

Jenny, leery of any plan that is accompanied by an evil grin like Fred has currently says, "Well lets hear it."

Fred, a little too excited says, "Well, I got a friend that has access to a box truck that we could use. Jenny, Sarah you guys know Dane. We've used it to haul the band gear and stuff around for when we want to shoot a music video. I'm waiting for him to text me back now. If we set up to shoot a video for the band, it should be enough of a distraction for you guys to get in and out with the stuff without them noticing."

Jenny, surprised by how much thought he put in on the fly says, "That's actually a great idea. It could possibly work."

Sarah, happy to be helping says, "I could post that we need a bunch of extras for the video. That way there would be so many people roaming around that you guys could move through the crowd unnoticed."

"Thanks, you know I do have good ideas on occasion." Fred says bewildered by how little confidence it seemed everyone has in him.

Seeing how Fred was taking it, I say, "Don't worry, you get use to it. At least they heard you out before telling you no. They voted and decided I'm not allowed to make plans without everyone approving first. So at least you got going for you."

"In Fred's defense, he only joined a bad group that tried to kill us. While you almost got us killed a few times." Jenny says.

A little offended, I say, "Hey, that flash mob thing was a stroke of pure genus."

Sebastian chuckles and says, "More like a genius that had a stroke." We all laugh. I even laughed more out of surprise that he came back so quickly with a burn. I've spent plenty of time around Sebastian and I think that has to be a first.

We all meander around while we wait for a response from Dane about the truck. Sebastian is sitting in his chair, inspecting the shotgun for any damages that I might have caused. Mother and Jacqueline flip the pictures a few more times to and try to match they ones they didn't know about up with images in a few of the old books. Fred sits and plays on his phone. Sarah wanted to look around the store for a while to kill time, and Jenny went with her to keep her company. This leaves me to sit in the corner.

Confused and as alone as I've felt in a while, I ponder these new gifts, as Mother keeps calling them. I have just as many questions as I ever did now. The list of abilities stacks up as the days continue. I ask myself all these things repeatedly, but only internally. It seems to be that this entire team dynamic is built around me. If it wouldn't have been for me wanting to venture out to a psychic fair, everyone would have been none the wiser. They would have been living that normal life that I never knew. As I get further into my self-hating, the voice of reason comes through into my head. It was Jenny speaking only to me, saying, "Suck it up. You may be part god or some shit, but I will blast your ass again if you don't knock this shit off."

Smiling to myself I say internally to her, "Yes ma'am. At least I got you out of this whole ordeal."

Fred stands up quickly, startling Mother says, "It's on. Dane is going to bring the box truck home from work. The others are down for a video as well. We are going to meet down there at 8 o'clock tonight, so be ready." Looking around the room, he sees Sarah and Jenny aren't in there. Yelling down the hallway, he says, "Sarah, get your people ready. Tell them to be there at 8."

Sarah's voice comes firing back down the hall, "On it!"

Sebastian takes Sarah to get a few things from her house while we wait. Fred leaves as well. He said he needed to get a few things for the video and meet Dane and Karl at their practice space to get the equipment.

Instead of standing around, Jacqueline has the idea to try to track down a few large bags. Jenny gets up and goes to help her so I can talk to Mother alone for a moment. She knows there is air that needs to be cleared between us. Most of the time I don't see what that girl sees in me, but I guess this destiny thing has its perks.

I not so subtly, plop into the chair across from Mother. Still looking through the books for references to the pictures I took says, "Spit it out child. I know there's something on your mind."

Not really knowing how to start, I decide the straightforward route is the best, and say, "What are you? I know what I saw and obviously you do as well. You always seem to know more than you want to say..."

Mother holds her hand up stopping me, and says "I'm going to stop you right there. For one, I don't know what you say, because there hasn't been anyone like you before. Nobody has ever been able to see others true nature or form. Secondly, yes I do know more than I'm saying because I want you to figure things out for yourself. Who I am is something that currently only one person knows, and no Sebastian isn't that person. The reason that I'm called Mother is harder to explain."

Perplexed by what I'm hearing, I say, "Well you can't just leave me hanging here. You knew that there was a family who watched me, watched Jenny. I know you are over a hundred years old at least. I have the pictures to prove it."

Mother, looked away for a moment to collect her thoughts. Finally she turns back and says, "If you're sure you can handle it, fine. I'm much older than a meager hundred years old, try several thousand. I was here before Christianity, before time, before there was a heaven and hell. In death my body was split into two, creating the heavens and the earth. This was all done by my own bloodline. That's when I vowed to return and reclaim my throne. I was reincarnated and have stayed hidden since then. I've watched you from a distance, always just out of reach. That is until you found your way to me on your own. I am your true mother."

Eyes wide in shock, I say, "What in the Babylonian hell are" I was cut short by Jenny and Jacqueline's return to the room and I say, "We will continue this later."

Mother in a half grin, whispers to me, "I'm sure we will my child, why don't you go sit down and cool off before you burn more clothes up."

Jenny sets down an armful of bags on the table. Sensing the tension in the room, she comes over and sits on my lap. Her hand on the back of my neck sends a chill through me, instantly making me focus on her. She knows she interrupted a rather intense conversation says, "So what's up, are we ready for operation - snatching the old shit?"

Being the smartass that I am, I say, "I'm ready. Mom, are you?"

Fuming, Mother says, "Ready as I will ever be, and never call me that again."

Confused, Jenny says, "I'm not sure I want to know what that's about, but you calling her mom, just sounds weird."

My smiling tipped Jenny off that I was keeping something from her, and Mother knows that there's no way this secret would be kept for long. Seeing Jacqueline leave the room, Mother takes the opportunity to say, "Jenny, I trust you will keep a secret that only two other people know. You are not to tell anyone, do you understand?"

Jenny knew from the way Mother was acting that had to be big, so she says, "Definitely. I won't say a word to anyone."

Leaning forward, in a low whisper Mother says, "I'm Jacob's real mother. He can fill you in on the other details later when you are alone."

With a snicker, Jenny says, "No need to wait for alone time, him and I talk all the time telepathically. I would've found out if he was hiding stuff from me eventually. That explains the mom comment, and his shitty attitude."

Sitting back in her chair, Mother says with a bitter tone, "So you two are inside each others heads completely now. How long has this been going on?"

I pass the list of my abilities I was making to Mother and say, "It's on the list, I was just trying to remember if I had forgotten any. Here check them out." Pointing onto the paper that Mother was holding I say, "See, right there. Number three, psychic link to Jenny."

Jenny looks at my list and asks, "Was I supposed to be making a list, or was it just your thing?"

Mother, looking up at Jenny from the paper says, "I guess you are both progressing pretty quickly. You two truly are meant for one another. No lists from either of you."

Taking the paper back, I crumble it up and say, "Fine, I won't keep track. Just figured it would help Catherine with her note taking thing. Oh yeah, we still need to cover that one of these days."
The text comes in from Fred saying that people are starting to show up. The plan is coming together nicely, but if I've learned anything from late nights television, it's that you should always have a backup or two ready to go.

Jenny knows how to get into the room if it comes down to it and we all might have a better shot at this if we split up into two teams. Sarah will stay with the band and crowd. She can text or call us if it looks like anyone is on to us. Sebastian can protect the others while I go at it alone. They are after me in the first place so I might as well capitalize on it.

Sebastian picks up Mother, Jenny and Jacqueline at the store. They head to the west bottoms while I get a ride with Sarah. As we pass over the bottoms on the 12th street bridge, I see the crowd gathering around the makeshift stage. There are people scurrying around with sound equipment and setting up lights.

We get about a block away and Sarah turns down a side street. This allows me to tuck and roll, so she doesn't have to stop the car. I dart into the shadows behind a dumpster and watch Sarah's car turn the corner. I think of Jenny, so she knows I made it, when I get a text from her. She says that they are in place and waiting for the music to start up.

Since I'm still a few blocks from the building, I start slinking my way through the alleyways to get closer. I stick to the shadows and near stuff I might be able to hide behind, which seems to be the right choice with the number of cops patrolling. Getting in the same way as before, wasn't an option now. They had to have that area under surveillance, or at least they should. I hear the roar of the crowd, and the blast of a guitar ring out through the speakers. The time has come.

On an adjacent building to where I need to go, I see a busted window on the ground floor. I take a running start and dive through. I hit the ground, rolling to my back in an effort to stay low. A spot light shines across the walls from a passing squad car checking the area. As the light vanishes, I focus my sight. I take in the surroundings, not a soul living or dead in my area. Getting to my feet, I need to find a way up to the roof.

Moving quickly down the hallways, turning here and there until I find the sign for the stairs. I need to make quick work of these so I can hop over the gap to the correct building.

I tell Jenny telepathically where I was as I run up flight after flight. The overwhelming stench of mold and vagrant homesteads fill my nostrils causing me to move faster. I didn't want to drag out my stay here if I didn't have to. Seeing a few figures pass by as I ran by the doorways, I knew they were no longer of the living. The fading outlines of the once alive, linger and fade into nothingness. They don't seem to notice, or care that I'm invading their space so I move on.

Rounding the last stretch of the stairwell, I see the roof door was halfway open. It appears to have been propped open with a brick, but I can tell that it wasn't recent. Probably so they could come and go as they wished, as well as let some of the funk out. Quietly, I work my way up the final few steps. Still focused, I look across to the next build. There as if it knew our plan, was the shadow figure waiting near the edge of the roof.

It must have seen me peeking out the door, because it holds it hand up to tell me to wait. Then it points down between the buildings. I walk slowly towards the edge wait. It waves me on a moment later. With a few steps, I leap the five foot space between the overhangs, landing firmly on the other side.

The shadow figure moves swiftly, causing me to sprint to keep up. It leads me to a skylight on the far west side of the rooftop. The lock on the skylight, rusted out long ago, made for easy access. I follow the figure through the opening and wait for it's next instructions. In my head I hear Jenny tell me they are in the build on the first floor hiding in the meat locker. I know that they could be stuck there for a while if I didn't do something.

Seeing a lone beam of light coming down the hallway, I see my opportunity to give them their chance to get free. Ducked down, I wait till the person gets closer. From his heavy footsteps, I know I need the element of surprise to take him down. Sliding silently closer to the door, I take one of the remaining daggers out of my jacket. Pushing the dagger into the top of the desk as a distraction, knowing the light will catch it as the man searches the rooms.

In the dust covered desk, I write look behind you. I crawl under the desk and wait. The vibration of of the mans footsteps radiate through the floor. Seeing the light on the wall behind the desk, I know he's close.

As I focus, I see the man standing right on the other side of the desk. He grips the handle of the dagger, with a solid tug, the blade pulls free of the desk. The man spins back and forth, looking around the room and says, "No use hiding. Come out and take your beating like a man. I got your message you left me on my guys chest. From what I hear you took out a few more of them with ease." Stabbing the blade back into the desk, hell yells "TRY THAT WITH ME, THE TWELVE WILL NOT FALL TO THE LIKES OF YOU!"

There was a creaking in the far corner of the room, causing him to turn. I lay on my back, and with my legs, I launch the desk airborne. It comes down on the mans back, knocking him to the floor. Quickly, I get to my feet and make a mad dash over the desk, landing just in front of him. Pulling the dagger from the desk, I immediately jam it through his hand, pinning it to the floor.

The man squirms to get free. Hate filling his eyes as he looks up at me. I can hear his anger and pain when he says, "The others will come for you, they will come in legions." The man coughs, blood flies from his lips as he struggles to breathe. "They will avenge me."

Flicking the dagger with my hand, causing the blood flow to increase I say, "Avenge you, avenge you? Who talks like that anymore? It's like saying you will rue the day. See that just sounds stupid. Anyway, back to the task at hand." I take his radio handset from his shoulder, and see the captains bars on the collar of his uniform shirt. "So you must be one of the top dogs in this Twelve thing. Well I guess there's only eleven more of you pukes to deal with. Just a little advice, if someone leaves a note in blood saying back off, you should probably do it."

Taking the dagger out of the floor, I look at the man as he slides his hand down to his belt. As his hand reaches his holster, I drive the dagger through his ear. The body twitches under the weight of the desk. Blood flowing from his ear and mouth, coating the floor.

Pulling the radio from his belt, pushing the talk button I say, "Hey, your boss doesn't looks so good. Somebody better come check on him." Laughing as I drop the radio.

Hearing the stomping rapidly approaching, I can tell my distraction worked. I run down the hallway towards the stairwell door. The pounding footsteps split off. A few follow me, and a few head to where I came from.

The echo of one of my pursuers sounds off, "The captains down, assailant is heading for the roof. Don't let him get away." A second later, I hear, "Copy that, we are in pursuit."

I burst through the rooftop door at the top of the stairwell, catching a younger officer off guard. I tackle him in mid-stride. Bringing him to the ground hard. With him unconscious on impact, I get up and run for the overhang. I make it to the edge as three more men clear the doorway, guns drawn and ready. I try to keep a pace just fast enough to get away, but not too fast to where I lose them. I want as many of them chasing me as possible. Hopefully Sebastian can take care of any stragglers that may have stayed behind.

Leaping to the next roof, I go down just over the edge faking an injury. It seems to have worked when the first of the three follows me over. I quickly take him to the ground, disarming him. The other two follow, opening fire as they land. I use the first one as a human shield, rolling him on top of me and letting his body armor absorb the impact of the rounds.

The firing stops for a moment as they reload. With everything I had, I shove the officer off of me, sending him tumbling at the first shooter. I grab a handful of gravel from the roof and throw it at the second. The riot helmet he's wearing protects his eyes but is clouded by the dust, buying me enough time to get to my feet.

Lunging forward, I spear the second man in the gut sending him staggering backwards off of the roof. Turning my attention to the other shooter, I see a man dragging a blade across his throat. The slow deliberate movement of his actions, tells me he isn't afraid of me or them.

The stranger releases his grip on the officer as the blood soaks the front of his uniform and says, "You have no need to fear me, my name is Cain. We need to talk."

I stand there confused, staring into his black eyes. Finally getting the nerve, I say, "Hey there Cain, I'm Jacob. Not sure if you can tell but I'm a little busy at the moment."

Standing as statuesque as anyone could possibly muster, Cain says, "I can see, where can I find you? We can talk tomorrow."

Annoyed by his lack of urgency, I say, "How about we meet up at the truck stop on K-32 for waffles tomorrow morning, say 9ish?"

Cain gives me a nod and steps off the roof. I hurry to the edge, looking over to see where he went to. Hoping to see a fire escape or a balcony just one floor down, but no. There was nothing. With the help of the street light, I see him round the corner on the sidewalk. My pondering is cut short by a round ricocheting on the stone lip just inches from my head.

I spin to my left to see four more armed officers running at full speed from the doorway. Knowing the next roof is weak, I make a break for it. I can survive a slight fall as far as I know, but I'm sure that that body armor can only take so much. They follow as I hoped they would, the problem is that they are gaining on me.

A clumsily jump into a combat roll to the next roof, allows me to increase my lead. The pitch black night sky hides the caved in area from this mornings escape. Finding the beam as I run, I put everything I have into this dash. The hard thud of the officers boots tell me they aren't too far behind. My foot pushes off the edge of the rooftop as a thunking sound rings out. I'm enveloped by a thick netting causing me to hit the rooftop hard, sliding to a stop. The four officers scream out as the roof gives way.

The sudden jerk of the net meant only one thing, they had a cable attached. The thought of getting this far only to be drug off of this roof pisses me off. My feet catch the stone lip, halting my demise. A radio that had fallen off of the officers chirps on the adjacent roof saying, "Any available officers, we have a female cornered on the third floor, black hair, mid to late 20's. Please respond."

Another voice rings out over the radio saying, "10-4, in route."

Hearing the description, my thoughts went to Jenny. My blood begins to boil, my skin gets hotter and hotter. Suddenly, I become engulfed in flames. My black onyx skin now glowed an orange-ish red, like molten rock. The netting burns and breaks, turning to ash upon contact with my flesh.

With everything going on, I didn't notice the two officers standing just seven feet away. I hear the metallic ping of the rounds being fired from the automatic rifles and wait for the impact. After a few seconds of waiting and feeling nothing, I turn to face them. The firing continues, allowing me to see the projectiles melt away as they get close.

I charge the two officers, reaching them in three steps. I swing wildly, impacting the trauma plate on the first man, collapsing it through his chest. With a back fist to the second man, his helmet flew of with his head still inside.

With the chase, I had forgotten Jenny and my connection. Screaming inside my head for her as I run back towards the other roof. As I jump, I hear her inside say, "We are safe, gathering the stuff now but we are going to need a distraction to get out."

Standing near the edge of the caved in roof top, I stare down at the rubble. The lights on the the officers uniforms show the devastation and carnage. One office lays still just to the side of the debris. My skin cools and returns to its normal onyx state, leaving me completely naked. The wheels turning inside my head, developing a plan that is both stupid and risky. Since that sums up my life, I feel it should work.

Jumping down in to the lower floor, careful not to create another cave in. I inspect the officers for signs of life. The three in the debris are done for, which was pretty easy to tell with rebar sticking through them.

The one that happened to roll to the side appears to have been knocked out from the fall. I kick his weapon out of reach in case he comes to and begin to strip him down. I make a pile of his clothes to one side, and his duty gear on the other. Using a set of zip cuffs, I bind his hands behind his back. At this point, I'm figure he's just playing out. Nobody would still be unconscious with as much as I've moved him around.

Getting dressed in the officers uniform, I realize how lucky I am to have found a guy close to my size to steal from. I mean the pants are a little snug on my junk but beggars can't be choosers. Gearing up with all of this equipment, I match where everything should go by checking the way it sits on the dead ones. With my face still visible, I notice that one of the men is wearing a mask under his helmet, letting only his eyes be seen. Putting the mask on I feel the wet, sticky remnants of blood causing it to cling to my face. Hopefully with the helmet the blood wont be visible.

Before I leave the room, I pick up a rifle so I appear more official. I make my way down to the ground floor to draw the others away from my team. Once outside, I key the mic on the radio and say in a muffled voice, "My teams down, I see the suspect. He's traveling south onto Jackson."

A voice answers on the radio, "Who is this?"

Looking at the name tag on the uniform, I say, "Page, Officer Page. The roof collapsed on us, the others are dead. I'm a little banged up but I'll live."

The radio goes off again, "Page, keep your distance but keep him in sight. Backup is on the way."

I key the microphone and say, "Copy that, I'll update on position." Hooking the microphone back to my uniform, I laugh to myself thinking that it might actually work. I hear Jenny inside my head telling me they are on the way out, so I hurry back to the building to meet them.

I pass a few officers that were standing guard near the rear of the building. I convince them that, I as Officer Page was in pursuit of me, and that I had gotten into the next building over. They fell for it, leaving it open for their escape. Just to give them more time, I head towards the stage area. I see several people slamming around in a mosh pit as the music blasts through the speakers. I toss my rifle into the back of the box truck and run straight for the crowd. Something about a man in full SWAT gear moshing sets the crowd on fire. A few officers notice what's going on and attempt to pull me out.

As the crowd swarms, I duck out of the chaos on my hands and knees. At some point my helmet is yanked off and is hoisted into the air. Once free, I make a break for the shadows under the bridge to hide. The black uniform helps conceal me in the darkness, giving me a chance to move from pillar to pillar searching for one of my friends cars.

It was my fifth set of cars before I found Jacqueline's car. Knowing they would need the space for all of the relics, I keep looking. Unable to find Sarah's car, I chance it and run back to the box truck. With all of the confusion, I climb into the back and hide under a furniture blanket.

I must have been more tired than I thought, because I'm jolted awake by something slamming down in the back of the truck. I pull the blanket to the side and see Fred loading drum boxes. I take the mask off and wave franticly hoping to catch his eye. He sees me just as Karl walks over carrying a large plastic tub. I cover myself back up quickly so I'm not seen.

Fred jerks the blanket off of me, and says, "Coast is clear bud, cops all took off in a hurry. Everyone is safe back at the store. You're free to catch a ride with us if you want."

Getting up off the ground, I say, "That would work, thanks. Let me help you guys load up. It's the least I can do."

"Damn right it is, from what I hear you owe me a shirt and some pants as well." Karl yells from outside the truck.

I jump down out of the truck and say ,"Hey Karl, yeah sorry about that. I'll add it to the list of things I owe people. I do have some pretty sweet riot gear if you're interested."

Rolling up wires, Karl looks over and says, "Hell yeah I'm interested. Hey Dane, guess what I'm wearing next show?"

Loading his bass into their cases, Dane looks up and asks, "What? I wasn't paying attention."

"Never mind, fuck him." Karl says tossing the bundle of wires in a bin.

"Come on over and I'll introduce you to everyone." Fred says, walking me towards the stage. Getting to where the others are Fred says, "That's Kylie, Eli, Dane and you know Karl."

Waving at everyone, I say, "Hey." The response was a mixture of smiles and head nods.

Karl passes by carrying a drum box says, "When Sarah said Jenny was dating a guy with black skin, I thought she was just being racist but damn dude what's up with your skin? I mean it looks like black rock or something."

I jog over to the truck to look in the side mirror when Fred says, "Yeah you did have skin there earlier. What happened with that?"

Staring at my reflection, I say, "I must have burned it off when I flared up. It was pretty bad ass."

"And now you look like a struck match." Dane says putting his cases in the back of the truck.

We get all the gear loaded and dropped off at the practice space. I climb into Fred's truck, after shedding the body armor. Karl wastes no time trying it on, helmet and all. I guess after it was pulled off my head, it had made its way to the stage where Karl had quickly snatched it up. Lucky for him, because now he has a complete set. Well, minus the automatic rifle. That thing is going with me.

On the drive back to the store, there was an uneasy silence in the truck. There has been several times that Fred would start to say something and stop before a word left his lips. I in return, sit there awkwardly gazing out the window, careful not to make eye contact. I've never exactly been a great conversationalist. I'm normally the one to say the wrong thing, or blurt out things that have no relevance to anything. I remember talking to Tim about the apartment the first time and for some reason brought up how I think honey is nothing more than bee vomit.

We sit through two lights, and working on a third when I say, "Dude, seriously just say what's on your mind. Whatever it is, it can't be as bad as you think. It's only going to get worse if you don't spit it out. Plus, the cars behind us are probably wondering why you haven't gone yet."

As Fred lets off the brake, he says through a shaken voice, "Where do I fit in?"

Confused, I say, "What do you mean, where do you fit in?"

Clearly agitated, Fred says, "Like in the group. It's not like I'm much use to you for intel on anyone other than my old group. I'm not special, like you, Mother, and the others."

With a laugh, I say, "Really, this is what has you all worked up? First off, you have helped more than you know, and not just with the intel crap. Secondly, we like having you around. At least I do, anyways. I know Jacqueline does, she would have been all alone without you watching after her. Let me tell you this. Being special isn't a great as you think. Think about it, I've gone through more clothes in the last month than most people do in five years. And, and technically I'm homeless and all my shit is destroyed."

Fred's smile let me know he was feeling better about his place in the team. We joke and laugh the rest of the drive about one thing and another. Not thinking, he parks right up in the stores parking lot. As we head around the back of the store, I hear Jenny yelling inside my head for me. I tell her to meet us at the door and let us in.

Greeted by Jenny at the door, without a word. I'm not even sure she noticed there was no skin on my face or head anymore. It is dark in the alley so I don't mention it. As we walk down the hallway she says, "So why's your phone going to straight to voice mail?"

Reaching for her as we walk, only to come up empty-handed, I say, "Sorry babe, it kinda melted. So did my clothes, actually. I was running around naked for a little while."

Walking through the curtains to the back room, Jenny says, "Serves you right." It hit her as she said it, turning to face me she says, "Wait, melted and naked." She sees my face as I clear the shadow. The human was now gone from my features, leaving the onyx demigod form completely visible.

She isn't the only one that notices either. The choir-like gasps reverb throughout the room. The shock to the others is frightening. After all we have seen these passed weeks, I couldn't have imagined that I would be the biggest of the freak shows.

Mother approaches, laying her quivering palm on my cheek. She ran her hand along my now stone-like jaw and says, "How? I mean, what happened while you were alone?"

Pulling away from her caress, I ask, "Do you want the long or short version of it?"

The novelty of the situation had worn off for Sebastian. As he went back to wrapping the handle on his new bone club says, "Great, no matter what we pick he's going to give us the long version."

Not wanting to get into all the details in the first place, I say, "Short version it is. Trying to distract them, I got caught in a net, got mad, covered in flames. Bye bye to clothes, and shit. Became bulletproof, stole a cops gear, ran into some dude named Cain, meeting him for waffles in the morning. Boom, done."

My bluntness gained me a few looks of distaste form the others. Mother grabs the broken antler from the pile of relics from the table and tosses it to me saying, "Well, if it's The Cain, you are going to want this. He will certainly be asking for it."

Looking over the antler, I ask, "Why? What's so important about an old antler?"

Mother shakes her head, clearly frustrated with me and says, "You really don't listen to anything but the sound of your own voice do you. That is the first blade. He used it to murder his own brother with it."

Tucking it into my cargo pocket, nonchalantly I say, "Oh cool. Well I'm meeting him at nine so if anyone wants to meet him, you are welcome to join us."

Jenny fires back in a tone riddled with attitude, "How do you suppose that's going to happen with the way you look, genius?"

Tired of always being thought lesser of, I say, "You know what, from the look of all of your faces when I came in here I'm just going to embrace it. No more hiding what, or who I am. This is me and if people don't like it, fine they don't have to be near me. That goes for each one of you as well. Now I'm going to find me a nice dark corner to crawl into and take a nap. Do with it as you will."

I storm off to the front of the store, grabbing the desk cover from one of the displays on the way by. I find a dark area near the east wall that was clutter free and lay down. I ball the dust cover up and tuck it under my head. A moment later, Jenny walks up. Curling up next to me, with her head on my chest.

We lay there quietly for a while, our breathing now in sync. She tilts her head up to look at me and says, "You know we just worry about you, right?"

Wrapping my arm around her, I say, "Yeah, I know. Are you okay with me looking like this?"

Snuggling up close, I can hear how tired she is as she says, "It's kinda hot, I got my very own demigod. Night babe, love you." She fades off to sleep.

Kissing her head, I say, "Love you too."

The morning sun sneaks it's way through a small crack between the plywood and window frame. The beam finds its target, landing directly in my eyes. Sitting up, it takes me a moment to shake the sleep from my mind. It was one of the most restful nights sleep that I can recall. Careful not to wake Jenny, I stretch and slowly stand up. No sounds of movement in the store to indicate that anyone else is awake. Moving silently through the clutter, I try to track down anything that might have the time. Remembering that Fred's laptop is in the backroom, I sneak back to see if it's still set up.

    Passing through the curtains, I see the laptop sitting near the edge of the table. Touching the mouse, the glow of the screen comes to life. From the looks of it, someone was cataloging the relics, as well as looking up things that they didn't know. The pile of relics has diminished from what I saw last night. They must have put the ones that they had already listed in the vault for safe keeping. I remember that this isn't my problem any longer and look in the bottom right corner of the screen for the clock, 6:03. Three hours to kill before the meet, and absolutely nothing to do.

The thought comes to me that I officially have no clothes besides the ones on my back. I sit back down at the table, sliding the laptop in front of me. The first thing that comes to me to search is military surplus stores. They tend to get in used uniforms and blood, dirt and grim is easier to hide in black and camo. I find one that's close to the waffle place and it opens in two hours. That gives me enough time to stop there before heading to meet Cain. I can't very well be walking around in a stolen SWAT uniform everywhere. It's bad enough that my skin and head look like a lava rock, but this thing will surely stick out. They will be on me within seconds.

I snatch my wallet out of the jacket I left here yesterday and see a box of shirts for the book store sitting against the wall. I take off the uniform top and toss it in the chair. I find my size shirt in the box and pull it on. Grabbing my jacket, I make my way to the door.

I hear movement behind me. Turning I see Jenny wiping the sleep from her eyes. As she stretches she says, "So I don't get waffles. Give me a sec to freshen up." She jogs off to the back room. It only takes her a minute before she comes out brushing her hair while putting her jacket on, purse dangling from the strap that she had clutched in her teeth. In a grunted voice she says, "Ready, lets go. Oh I snag Jacqueline's keys so we don't have to hoof it."

I follow her out the door, locking it behind us. She unlocks the car and jumps into the drives seat. I know arguing with her is pointless, so I climb in the passenger side. I explain to her where I was wanting to go first before we get food, and she says she knows right where to go. We drive without saying a word. I can't lie to her since she can see inside my head. Honestly, this is one of the first times my thoughts have been calm and quiet. She reaches over gripping my hand. This peaceful moment is what I want for us. None of the fights, the random attack, the killer gods or devoted cults. This right here. One day I will give her this, even if it means that we have to leave everything else behind. We stayed this way the rest of the drive to the surplus store.

Parking the car, she says, "Are you sure you want to do this? I can just run in and grab some stuff for you if you want."

Feeling surprisingly free, I open the door and say, "No, I'm good. I can't just go around hiding all the time and making you do everything for me." She sees my mind is made up and gets out. Joining me on the passenger side, we lean against the car.

The open sign clicks on after waiting for thirty minutes. We walk to the door, hesitating for a moment as I reach for the door. The jitters set in, but only for a brief time. She places her hand on my shoulder, giving me that boost I need. Pulling the door open, I take that first step inside.

It took a second for the cashier to notice me before I hear him say, "Dear God man. What the hell happened to you?"

Me being use to coming up with things on the fly, I say, "Honestly dude, I have no clue. The VA says it's a reaction to some of the chemical weapons that we encountered over in the sand box. Turned my whole body black as night and hard as a rock."

Embarrassed by asking, the cashier says, "I'm sorry, I shouldn't have asked. Thank you for your service. Oh all vets get a discount, if you find something you like just let us know. I'm sure we can help you out."

I nod, and say "Thanks, I could sure use it. You know those disability checks never go as far as you need them to." Then I walk off.

Jenny and I browse the isles. Up one and down another. Finally we come across the used clothes near the back of the store. Out of the five racks of clothes we find four pants and five shirts. The prices are faded and hard to read, so I just grab them all. On the way back to the front, I pick up a couple of packs of undershirts.

Setting them on the counter, I say, "The prices are hard to read, how much are these? Oh and can I get one of those black riggers belts as well?"

The guy looks through the clothes, and after typing it all into his calculator he says, "I'll make you a hell of a bargain. Forty-five for all of them and when we get more stuff in your size, we can give you a call. That way you don't have to wonder if we have stuff in your size."

"You got a deal, sir. Babe, can you give him your number please? My phones broke remember." I say, pulling out my wallet. I pay and we head to the car. We only have ten minutes to get to the waffle place. Jenny says she can get us there in five, so I let her do her thing. I have no clue how to get around in this city, without her to get me places it would take me forever to get anywhere. We cruised in to the restaurant in time to see Sebastian and Mother get out of Fred's truck.

Silently, we all walk into the lobby where we are greeted by a woman of her fifties. She seems to not have a care to give. I see Cain sitting at a booth in the rear of the diner. Taking Jenny's hand, I walk us pass Mother and Sebastian. We slide into the booth across from Cain, while Mother and Sebastian take the booth across the isle from us.

Everyone orders, except for Cain. He continues to drink his cup of black coffee. Not bothered by my appearance, he says, "I see you shed the last of your human skin. That's good, it suits you."

I give a smug look to Mother, looking back to Cain I say, "Thanks, I like it." Reaching into my cargo pocket, I pull out the broken antler. Sliding it across the table to him I say, "I believe this is yours."

Taking the antler off of the table and tucking it into his inside pocket, Cain says, "I appreciate that, but it's not why I said we needed to talk."

Surprised, I say, "Oh okay, then why did you want to meet?"

Sipping his coffee, he looks at the others. Setting his cup down, he says, "You keep interesting company. I can't believe how long it has taken you two to finally be together. It seems like just yesterday that I was in Jerusalem watching you run after her carriage."

Shocked, Jenny says, "So that was real, we thought it might have been some weird dream."

"It was most definitely real. The fact that there have been countless times that I witnessed your fates intertwine, only to be snuffed out by one faction or another." Cain says as stone faced as if someone was telling you what color the grass was.

I laugh to myself, thinking that all of those dreams, all of those books back at Catherine's, all of those people out there. They all have one thing in common, they are all trapped in the past. There is nothing anyone can say or do that will tell them what I'm going to do next.

I see Cain notice my half grin, so I say, "So, Cain what is it that you needed?" Our food arrives and as it's passed in front of me, I say, "It can't be the company and amazing food."

He waits for the waitress to walk off, then he says, "The reason I'm here is to let you know who you are dealing with. These aren't just a few nut jobs that like to play dress up. They are actually under the orders of the church. Their orders come straight from Vatican City. The Order of the Twelve dates back since the first Crusaders in 1095. Even when the Templar were disbanded, the church kept this order secret. Their sole purpose is to retrieve holy items for the church's archives."

Digging into my food, between bites I say, "Great, fanatics. Well the Order of the Twelve needs to rename themselves to the eleven. I took out one of them last night."

"I wish it was that easy, but there is always someone waiting to take their place. They are always more devoted and more willing to serve than the last. The younger ones tend to rush in guns blazing. They don't what you are capable of since all of the ones you came across haven't survived to pass on your skills. Currently, they think you are just an annoyance that's hard to kill." Cain says

Jenny, thinking back says, "But they know he's a demigod. They put it in the note."

Refilling his cup with the coffee pot that was left on the table, Cain says, "They weren't thinking of him when they wrote that note, it was meant for you. They didn't even know Jacob was involved until he got in the middle of it."

Confused Jenny says, "I'm not a demigod, I just have abilities. Nothing like Jacob."

Cain glances over at Mother and back at Jenny and says, "I'm guessing she didn't tell you the full story. Well, I will give you the short version. I'm sure she can fill you in on the rest later. The reason you two are drawn to be together, is simple. You are part of each other. You were once one and now two separate beings built of the same. The heavens are crowded with gods and on occasion they join together to make beings that walk the earth. I myself am also the result of their boredom. We are nothing but their discarded toys."

Sarcasm covering up the level of shock, I say, "Wow, I thought I had parental issues." Seeing the line went over like a ton of bricks, I say, "So if her and I are the same, why do we have different abilities?"

Breaking her silence, Mother says, "Because the gifts were split between the two of you. You, Jacob have more of your fathers gifts, while Jenny has more of mine."

Jenny, chocked on her food for a second when she hears Mother's reveal. In my tactless nature, I say, "Mother of the year everyone. So should I stop banging my sister or is it not like that?"

I catch an elbow to the ribs from Jenny before she says, "So you knew this entire time and didn't say anything. If you're my mother than who the hell was I raised by? And does this mean that we are brother/sister or what?"

Cain still as stone faced says, "You aren't brother and sister, you are soul mates. In the beginning, everyone had a partner that was created just for them. The special ones were made from one another, like you two."

The relief cascades over Jenny and I both. The thought at what we have done would have decimated any chance of eye contact much less working as a team. Jenny says, "Thank God, or gods or whatever for that."

Smiling, I load up my fork with my now cold waffles I say, "That would have made family dinners awkward. Hey mom, I think I knocked up my sister."

The look of hatred comes my way from Mother, as she says, "This is nothing to joke about."

Sebastian, who has been sitting quietly through all of this says, "So if you are their mother or whatever, who is the other half of them?"

Mother, frustrated with the questions says, "It wasn't a man at all, he was an angel that helped me in the beginning. That's why your gifts are so unpredictable. There has never been an offspring from an angel and a God before. He has been known by many names. Lucifer is what you might know him as."

I burst out laughing. Catching my breathe I say, "So dear old dad is the Devil. You did have a bad streak back in the day didn't you?" The look that Mother gives me is of pure hate.

Sebastian, with a mouthful of food says, "That explains a lot." Hearing that almost made me spit waffles all over Cain. I'm not sure if it was a shot at me or Mother, but it was funny regardless who it was intended for.

Between sips of his coffee, Cain says, "Lucifer wasn't such a bad guy in the old days. He was the chosen one, his favorite. Well, until that rebellion thing. He still owes me, but that's another story for another time."

Finishing my food, I push the plate to the side and say, "So what's your deal, how or why are you still around?"

Cain must be use to answering this question, because it took him no time to say, "It's my punishment for killing my brother. For that I was sentenced to be the executioner for the heavens. Worst part is that I'm not allowed to die. Complete bullshit. They send a hit list and I send souls."

Jenny stirring her coffee say, "That must be so lonely."

"After a few thousand years, you get use to the solitude." Cain says.

We finish up and pay. Cain leaves on foot, while we follow Mother and Sebastian to drop off Fred's truck at his work. The four of us ride back to Jacqueline's in complete silence. It was that awkward quiet that leaves everyone on edge. Sebastian, feeling betrayed for not knowing any of this after the many decades of helping Mother. Mother, ashamed by the fact the secrets are out. Jenny, uneasy and confused finding out her entire life had been a lie. Then there is me. Mom is the god of the Sumerian gods and Daddy-o is the first of the fallen. What does that even make me? Was he an angel at the time or the head demon? I doubt that Mother will ever say but I'm sure it won't come up at Christmas dinner.

I zoned out for a while during the drive, lost in my own little world. I haven't paid any attention until we are parked and I get out of the car.

Expecting to see Jacqueline's place, I'm surprised when I see the cell phone store. Jenny tosses the keys to Sebastian and lets them know we will walk back after I get a new phone. I feel sorry for Sebastian. He is as much, if not more, of a pawn in this mess as we are. He as her protector, and Jenny and I to help Mother regain her throne. What she doesn't realize is that the old ways are gone. Most people walking around either don't care for any of the thousands of gods out there or are stuck in some bastardized version of a religion that has forgotten what the original purpose was to begin with.

Splitting ways for the moment was needed. There are so many things Mother, Mom, Mommy-dearest has kept from us all. It takes Cain of all people to walk in, drop a bomb, and walk out to get a few things out in the open. Jenny explains to the salesman my phone was lost in a fire. Good thing about all of this is that I was due for an upgrade. So I get a free phone out of the deal.

We start back to the store, taking the long way to give us a minute to ourselves. Jenny's phone goes off, and from her expression it wasn't good. She takes off at a sprint, leaving me to guess what's wrong. Instead of questions, I just run.

Rounding the corner at the end of the block, my run is halted as I'm yanked to the the side by Sebastian's massive paw. I had enough time to see Jacqueline on a stretcher being loaded into the back of an ambulance. The four of us wait in the alley, peeking at the crime scene like spectators. With every badge in the city, as far as we know, after us. There is nothing we can do.

From my vantage point, I see an officer speaking to a girl. I recognize the girl from my first visit to the store. She must be a regular that happened to see what transpired. She is who we need to talk to. Me in my current state, would probably scare the hell out of her so Jenny volunteers. The girls are close to the same age and hopefully Jenny can find something, anything out about what happened.

While Jenny sneaks over, I text Fred. I'm sure he will want to know what's going on. It seems that he and Jacqueline have become close friends if nothing else, over the last few weeks. Only a few minutes pass, when Jenny and the girl walk into the alley.

"Hey everyone, this is Beth. Beth, this is Sebastian, Mother, and that's Jacob." Jenny says pointing us out.

A little skittish, Beth says, "Hey. I've seen you around the store before. Jackie use to let you in through the back. And didn't you have skin the last time?"

Intrigued that she remembered who I was, I say, "Yeah, that's kind of a long story. So what happened to her, we just saw her a few hours ago."

Looking back towards the store front, Beth says, "Like I told the cops, I came by to see if the store was open for business yet, and I went to the back to knock on the door. When I got back there the door was open, so I went in. When I got to the end of the hall I saw three guys in masks beat Jackie. When they saw me they took off."

Thinking the story over in my head, I say, "You said they were wearing masks, what did the masks look like?"

Reaching for her pocket, she says, "I managed to snap a picture before they saw me. I didn't tell the cops about it because they didn't seem to concerned with knowing what happened." She scrolls through the phone and says, "See, right here."

"Can you send that to me?" I ask. She obliges my request.

The masks were all white with a red cross on the side. The Knights attacked an unarmed woman. My anger starts to build. As I try to calm down I say, "We will take care of the guys that did this, don't worry. Do you know how badly she was hurt?"

Still shaken, Beth says, "It was hard to tell, there was a lot of blood. I did hear them say that they were talking her to the hospital on 23rd street."

Jenny notices the girls unease during the questions says, "Hey Beth, why don't you take off and we will take care of stuff here. Maybe we will see you at the hospital later." Beth gives her a nod, and walks back to her car.

The four of us look at one another, lost and confused. The only thing that makes sense right now is to cause them as much pain as possible, and I think I know right where to start. I convince Jenny to take Mother to the hospital, while Sebastian and I check on a lead. The ladies only seem to go along with it because I have Sebastian here. They believe that he will keep me out of trouble. From the look he had when he watched Jacqueline being loaded, I know there won't be any resistance to dealing out a little justice. Once separate from the other two, I lay my plan out for Sebastian.

Riding to the first stop in the cab seems to take forever. We left the downtown area and were deep into the suburbs. The manicured lawns adorn every property. The flower gardens in full bloom around the homeowners association signs on the corner. Arriving at our destination, I pay the driver and step out to take in the clean suburban air and the picturesque white picket fence having split level ranch. The chiseled stone displays the name I was looking for, Hatch Family.

Checking the surroundings, I only see a few cars in driveways and not a soul outside. Sebastian and I head to the door as inconspicuous as we can muster, to not draw any attention to ourselves from the watchful eyes of nosy neighbors. Standing at the door, we hear music coming from inside. I ring the doorbell, stepping to the side so all they will see when looking is Sebastian.

The door opens. Officer Friendly stands there, dumbfounded with a sandwich hanging half out of his mouth. The grin that Sebastian has on his face as he forces his way in, is priceless. Creepy as hell, but priceless. I follow Sebastian through the door. I wasn't paying attention to how he got on the floor, but the good officer was on the ground doing some crab walk thing trying to get away. In two steps, the big man caught up to Officer Hatch. Snatching him up with one hand, Sebastian tosses him into a nearby chair.

Sitting on the coffee table in front of Steven, I say, "There's no need for me to restrain you, is there? If I'm correct you are just going to sit there like a good little snitch and tell us everything we want to know." I give a nod to Sebastian, who pulls out his bone club from under his jacket. "Or you can not tell us things and my large friend here will break everything he sees, and yes that includes you."

On that cue, Sebastian swings the club down hard on a solid wood end table, sending splinters flying in all directions. The explosion of wood causes the officer's bladder to empty. I try my best to hold in my laughter with no luck. My laughter, mixes with the sounds of his sobs to make a symphonic balance of horror.

Calming myself down, I say, "I'm sure you know why we made this little visit. In case you don't let me refresh your memory." The radio is shattered by the club. Looking up at Sebastian, I say, "Dude really, I'm trying to ask him questions."

Sebastian shrugs and says, "Sorry, I hate that song."

Shaking my head, I go back to talking to the hostage. "Okay, where was I? Oh yeah, the reason we are here. A friend of our was recently attacked by a couple of goons that are in your little group. You know the ones I'm talking about. They have the red cross, on a field of white."

Steven turns his head to try to get a look at where Sebastian is, and says, "I've been here, they don't trust me anymore since you carved me up. I swear, they haven't told me anything." Sebastian took that as a reason to smash the wall mounted flat screen TV. The sparks shoot out from the shattered screen.

Careful not get up, Steven dodges the airborne glass, and crying out says, "I SWEAR, I DON'T KNOW ANYTHING ABOUT AN ATTACK!"

"But you know who does, and that's what we're here for. All this can stop, if you just give us what we ask for. At the rate he's breaking shit, he will probably be moving on to you any time now." I say, brushing off the broken glass from my sleeve.

"Alright, alright. I'll make you a list of every one of them that I know of, just please stop." Steven says out of fear.

Patting his leg, I say, "See, I knew we could come to an agreement. Now where do you keep your paper and pens?"

He points to the left side of the room at a small desk, and says, "Over there, top drawer."

Sebastian walks over to the desk. With a massive downward swing of the club, the desk crumbles. Sending the contents to scatter and clutter the floor. As Sebastian kicks through the rubble, I chuckle and say, "Geeze, was that called for?"

Handing me the paper and pen, Sebastian says, "No, but it felt good."

I pass the items to Steven to make the list, and say, "Fair enough."

Officer Hatch made his list. From the looks of it, he was giving up anyone and everyone that could've been involved in this mess. It takes him a good twenty minutes to write it out. There were names, addresses, phone numbers, and even a few emails. Not sure why I might need email addresses, but I figure he was too scared to leave anything out this time, for fear we might come back.

On our way out the door, I turn and say, "Do you mind if I borrow your car? I promise not to scratch it. It's just I spent the last bit of cash on the cab ride out here."

Exhausted from the questions, Steven had no fight in him and says, "You know what, I don't care anymore. Just take it."

I take the keys off the hook by the front door, jingling the keys I say, "Thanks man, it helps a lot. Oh, if anyone asks what happened, tell them it was a home invasion." I give Sebastian a wink, causing him to catch Hatch with a right cross on his way by. The crunch of bone and splatter of blood, sends the officer reeling to the floor unconscious.

After taking the guys car, Sebastian and I decide to start working our way through the list, beginning with the ones with addresses. I let the big man drive since if I were driving, we would be completely lost. For someone who's lived in this area for as long as I have you would think that I would know where things were. I guess being a hermit for most of my time has really caught up to me.

Truthfully, I enjoy the hermit life. Nobody to worry about, nothing trying to kill you. It was kind of peaceful. I was nice that Steven let us take his car. Even better that it had a full tank. Scrolling through the list, I see that three of these guys live at the same address, so we head there. What's odd is that the officer that I stole my wardrobe from last night isn't on the list. I guess it was a good thing that I left him alive.

Sebastian parks across the street from the first address. It's a large two story place with an unattached garage to the right of it. The garage door is sitting open and we can see there is only one car inside. The car is one of those small foreign jobs that they use in the street racing drift movies. The way the tools are laid out, it looks like someone is either about to work on it or they just finished. Either way, it doesn't matter. It means someone is home.

We sit and wait, hoping that someone comes back outside. We aren't kept waiting long before a younger man returns to the garage. He slides a large hydraulic jack under the front end of the car and jacks it up. Once on the jack stands, the man climbs underneath.

To avoid being seen, we walk on the far side of the driveway away on the opposite side of the open garage door. We slip quietly into the garage through open door. With one swift motion, Sebastian took hold of the mans ankles and jerked him from under the car. Before the man had a chance to react, I straddle him and drop with all of my weight onto his chest. His body tenses as the air escapes his lungs.

As I stare down on the guy, the thought crosses my mind that he seems younger than the others. Flicking him on the forehead, I say, "Hey there Shrimp, you look a little on the young side to be a religious fanatic."

Staining under my weight, he asks, "Who are you people? What do you want from me?"

Bouncing up and down on the kids sternum, I say, "Oh come on, you know why we are here. If you want, my big friend here can ask you. To warn you, he isn't as friendly as I am."

Panicking, the guy says, "Did Tony send you, is this about the race? I got his cut over there, I just had to get the car running right before I dropped it off."

Now confused, I get up from his chest and say, "What the hell kid, what kinda shit are you mixed up in? Get up." I pull him up from the ground and shove him back into the car.

In his bewilderment, he says, "So you aren't Tony's guys"

"No, we aren't Tony's or anyone's guys for that matter. What's your name?" I say, getting agitated.

The kid wipes the grease off of his hands with the shop towel hanging out of his pocket, and says, "Jim Ellis Jr, but everyone calls me JJ."

Looking back at the list, I ask, "Is your dad a cop or something by chance?"

The confusion on his face slowly changes to relief and then to fear, as he says, "Yeah, he's a sheriff's deputy. Why, what do you want from him?"

"Look JJ, it doesn't matter what we want from him. What matters is if you are willing to tell us where he and his buddies are." I say, folding the list back up and cramming it down into my pocket.

Fear was front and center on the kid as Sebastian steps closer. Taking a defensive stance, JJ says, "I'll tell you where they are just don't hurt me. He's a dick anyway."

Sebastian leans in and says, "You better not be lying kid, because if you are I will come back here and choke you out with your own spine."

Visualizing that in my head, I shake off the thought and say, "Unfortunately he's serious, so spill it."

JJ gives us more details than we know what to do with. He tells us everything from his work shifts, to where his dad and buddies favorite watering hole is at.

"Hey, why are you telling us all this, aren't you afraid we are going to hurt him when we find him?" I say.

"Afraid, no. More like hoping you hurt him. I'm only here because the court says he gets me every other weekend. Those assholes make me sleep on the couch while they have the spare bedroom full of their history crap." JJ says. The anger in his voice comes through like a freight train.

Sebastian gives me an excited glance, and says, "Show us this room, if you would."

Following JJ into the house, he takes us through the kitchen and shows us a door with two rather serious looking security locks keeping it closed. I see Sebastian pull the massive bone club from his jacket. Knowing what is coming next, I push JJ against the wall and shield my eyes. The impact of the bone on the metal locks, sent shards flying. Tucking his club back away with one hand, Sebastian pushes the remaining part of the door open. Waving me in, I stroll into the room.

The walls are adorned with three shields, baring the red cross on a field of white. Armor and mid-evil weapons clutter the floor. Some on stands, while other just tossed carelessly into a pile. In the corner of the room I find what I was hoping for. There in a bundle of blood stained clothes, I see the masks. The clothes and masks match the ones from the picture that Beth had taken of Jacqueline's attackers. I pick up the masks and hand them to Sebastian to hold on to.

Feeling my rage building, I say, "You two might want to leave the room, I have something that I need to take care of and you wont want to see it."

Sebastian takes JJ out into the hallway to watch after him. I strip down and toss my clothes in to the doorway. The fire inside begins to burn hotter and hotter until my onyx shell turns molten. Placing my hand on the first shield, the metal melts, dripping onto the floor. I move systematically through the room destroying every piece of Templar crap I see. Once all it has been reduced to clumps of smoldering scraps, I calm myself. It only takes a few moments before the orange-ish red hue of my skin, returns to its glassy onyx. I get dressed and meet the other two back in the hallway.

Sebastian gives me a questioning glare, and I say, "Let go, I'll tell you in the car." With that, we head back outside.

I explain to JJ, it's probably in his best interest to get his car going and get the hell away from the house for a while, and to stop owing money to people that might send people like us to hurt him. From the blank look on his face, I assume it was a waste of my breath. Sebastian and I head back to the car so we can get on the road to the next stop.

I check the time to see how long we've been away from the girls. It's been almost three hours with no update on Jacqueline's condition. My anxiety must be wearing off on the big man, because he checks his phone as well. We agree to make this next stop, our last for the day so we can get to the hospital. No information is not always a good thing when it comes to hospitals. Usually it means complications or they won't tell anyone the prognosis unless you are family. As far as I know, none of us are family, but I could be wrong. I didn't know until this morning that my bio-dad is the Devil either, so there's always a chance.

Sebastian parks the car directly in front of the bar that JJ told us about. At this point in our journey, being subtle is not at the top of our list. When you're dealing with religious fanatics you need to go to the extreme to get through to them. When those fanatics also happen to carry badges, there's no point in hiding. It's time to stop playing cat and mouse, and take the fight to them on their turf. I have Sebastian wait in the car so we can make a quick getaway if needed. I take the mask from him and put it on. Checking my reflection in the mirror, I decide that I resemble a bad wrestler more than anything. I put my hood up and get out of the car.

From the outside of the place, it looks like an Irish pub that is well passed its prime. The windows packed with neon beer lights, some worked and some didn't. The open sign flickers revealing its age and use. One tug of the door shows me that they don't follow the no smoking policy that the city put in place a few years back, as the smoke cloud billows out. Keeping my head down as I enter, draws immediate attention.

Not even three feet inside when a yell rings out from across the room, "We're closed!"

Being the mouth that I am, I say, "The sign says open, and there's an awful lot of people in here to be closed."

The voice from before says, "Private party, and you're not on the guest list."

I tilt my head up and pull off my hood to reveal my mask, and say, "See, I was told I was on the list. Oh well, I guess I'm going to report back that the location was wrong."

At the sight of the mask, several of the patrons straighten up and become more aware. A man in uniform gets up from the bar and walks towards me. As he gets closer, I see he has lieutenant bars on his collar.

The lieutenant reaches his hand out to shake mine, and says, "I didn't realize our call for back up would come so quickly, but the mask isn't necessary in here. You are surrounded by friends of the cause."

I shake his hand, then reach up to take off the mask and say, "That's exactly what I wanted to hear."

Peeling of the mask, the neon's reflect off my onyx head. As if by slow motion, every ones reaction time froze to a crawl. Taking advantage of their shock, I catch the lieutenant with a solid left hook in the jaw. He tumbles to the ground as the others made their choices whether or not to run or charge. Gripping the chair to my right, I swing it taking out a middle-aged man that was reaching into his jacket. Dodging a few bottles that were thrown, I move closer to the few that stand their ground. I shed my jacket and grab a bottle from a table in one motion. I smash the bottle on the edge of the bar and stab the bartender in the neck, just as the bat he had under the bar cleared the cooler. I take the bat and work over a large man that was charging while my back was turned. The knife he dropped as he fall would make Rambo jealous. As the last man fell, I turn my attention to the lieutenant. He was crawling on his belly behind the bar, by the time I make it to him.

He draws his pistol and clumsily fires two rounds. The shots go wide missing me by a foot, minimum. The shot to his jaw has left him unable to see straight. I take the pistol from his hand and toss it behind me to keep it out of his reach. Taking my left foot, I place it on the red swelling side of his jaw. Slowly, I apply pressure until his gargled cries spew from his crimson coated lips.

I snap back to why I'm here, information. Releasing the pressure, I say, "I'm going to ask you questions, and you are going to answer them. There's no chance you will survive this without injury. But there is chance of making it out alive."

I grab a bottle of vodka from the shelf nearest me and as I pour it on his face, I say, "First question, how many of the 12 are here in KC?"

His eyes get wide as I pick up a book of matches. As I strike one, he says, "Only two, only two per city. The rest are followers. Please don't kill me." He says through his sobs.

Watching the match burn, I say, "Next. Who ordered the attack on the woman at the book store?"

"That came from above, from the church. They were just supposed to scare her. She fought back and stabbed one of the guys." The lieutenant says, keeping his eyes on the flame.

Smiling, I say, "Good, he deserved it. Once I find him a little stab wound will be the least of his worries. Third and final question for you. How many of you do I need to kill to get you to back off?"

"I can call them right now and tell them, nobody else needs to die." He says pulling his phone from his pocket.

Backing up to give him space, I say, "You go ahead and make that call, I'll wait."

In seconds he is on the phone. From all the yes sirs he was sputtering he was talking to someone further up the food chain. I snatch the phone from him and say, "Who's this?"

The voice thick with Italian says, "Who is this, what happened to Lieutenant Ellis?"

Satisfaction of who I had on the floor, makes me grin as I say, "Depends on what name you know me as, but that doesn't matter. The reason I called was to let you know that the Twelve are no longer needed in my city. I've already take out at lease twenty or thirty of your followers, and it's starting to annoy me. Now I'm going to give the phone back to Jim Sr over here and you can tell him to pack his shit and move out."

I pass the phone back to Ellis. He looks up at me as he is being told something on the phone. I take my gloves off and push up my sleeves. Concentrating on my hands, I feel them start to heat up. The skin on my hands turns cherry red. Touching Lieutenant Ellis with both hands on his vodka soaked shirt, he is engulfed in flames. I know the screams are coming through loud and clear to the man on the other end of the phone, since I see the screen still lit up, showing connected.

I dip my hands into the ice bin to cool them off. I dry the off as I step over his burning body. I pick up my gloves and jacket on my way out the door. I remember the huge knife that the one man dropped, and go back to get it. Tucking it into my jacket, I kick open the door. The sun has started to set while I had been inside. Getting in the car, I wave for Sebastian to drive.

Pulling away from the bar, Sebastian asks, "So, did the boy's story check out?"

Buckling my seat belt, I sigh and say, "You could say that. They thought I was the backup that they had called in."

Watching traffic as he waits to make a left turn, Sebastian says, "So that means we have company coming, any clue on how much? I would like to be able to plan accordingly."

Shrugging, I say, "No, but I talked to some snooty Italian guy. I explained why it would be in his best interest to call off the dog or to stock up on coffins."

It remains quiet for a minute. We both know they are coming and they will probably be better equipped than the locals. The realization of the certainty of a war between these guys is tiresome. I don't want to lose any of my small group of friends. Jacqueline is the first casualty, and we don't even know how she's doing. The hospital is within sight, and the worst possible scenarios play over in my mind.

I tap Sebastian with the back of my hand, and say, "I almost forgot, I got you a present at the bar."

Sebastian shoots me a surprised look, as I reach into the inner pocket. Pulling out the massive blade, I say, "I saw it and thought of you. One of the guys dropped it and I figured why not."

Sebastian looks over the knife. Taking in the twelve inch blackened steel blade. The handle is a rubber grip, with finger groves set into a set of spiked brass knuckles. His gorilla paws fit just right as he tests the weight and balance. Even though the big man didn't say anything, the smile he had was thanks enough. Tucking it under the seat as we pull into the hospital parking lot, he give me a nod.

Before we head in, I reach out to Jenny internally. The number 318 pops into my head. Sebastian walks right in the front door, and waves me in. There's no security watching the door, so we head straight for the elevator. The less questions the better, when you look like me. The elevator arrives, and is empty. The lack of people is a little concerning, especially for this being the gun shot and knife wound center for the city. The doors close and we start ascending two the third floor. The ding of the bell sounds on the second floor. As the door opens, I see a sea of uniforms waiting.

Shoving Sebastian to one side as I jump backwards to the other. A canister glides across the floor, and explodes as it hits the back wall of the elevator. Tear gas and smoke fill the compartment, hindering sight. Lucky for me, my gift kicks in and allows me to see through the cloud. The first man enters, barreling straight ahead. His riot shield angled to shovel one of us into a corner, protects his body. Holding my breath, I circle behind him, ripping the gas mask from his face. Tossing the mask to Sebastian with one hand, leaving the man gasping for air. I wrap my arm around the mans neck in a rear chock hold. Controlling his body, I spin him causing him to drop the shield. Sebastian quickly retrieves the shield and prepares for the next one to enter. I move closer to the door and hit the door close button. The door starts to close and I charge forward, allowing it to close behind me. Sebastian knows that his job is to protect the girls and I will clear out this mess.

Standing by the elevator doors, I see at least ten men in uniform all baring the Templar's cross. They weren't approaching, only surrounding me. The smoke begins to dissipate, giving them no reason for the gas mask any longer. I remove my jacket and gloves, tossing them to the side. I feel my skin begin to heat, as I say, "So are we going to do this, or what?"

A tall man in front of me say, "Your kind can not harm us demon. The church and the heavens are our saviors."

I let out a laugh as my onyx flesh turns red. Grabbing the man to my right, his uniform burst into flames. I swing his body in front of me as another fires a shot from a shotgun. The burning mans screams cease as the round enters his ribcage. I release his inflamed corpse, sending it into the men on my left. As they dodge the body, I kick the man in front of me hard in his trauma plate sending him to the ground on his back. Careful not to stay in one spot so they can't shoot at me again, I dart for another man tackling him hard. The body armor smokes and sparks into flame, cooking the man inside his protective gear. The remaining men took off at a sprint for the stairs. I can see that they've had their fill of the brutality, since none of their efforts have worked. I walk over to the man I had kicked, cooling off as I got closer. I needed to know what was going on, and setting him on fire before I even start won't get me anywhere.

He winces in pain from the kick he received. I squat down next to him and say, "So you must be the reinforcements, I guess they failed to mention what it was you were coming to deal with." I drag him over to the wall and prop him upright. I see a chair close by and roll it over to sit in while we talk.

Between his haggard breathes, he says, "What are you?"

Sitting down in front of him, I say, "That's an interesting question, with an even more interesting answer that you will never know. So why are you here?"

Pulling weakly at the straps on his vest, he says, "We were sent for the relic, that the girl has."

Confused, I say, "What relic, she doesn't have any relics, I think the higher up need to check their intel before they mess with people."

Struggling to remove his gear so he could breathe easier, he says, "It's something that was given to her by..."

A shot rings out, causing me to instinctively dive for cover. Looking towards where the shot came from, I see a person decked out in full tactical gear, with a Templar mask on. He falls back into the stairwell, with the door closing behind him.

Now that the coast is clear, I return to check the man I was talking to, only to find him dead. There was a well placed round buried in between his eyes. With that kind of aim, the shot wasn't meant for me, but to shut him up. You know it's serious when they start taking out their own people. I've wasted enough time here. Since they are still in the building, I need to get to Sebastian and the girls.

I gear up with the crap that this last group left behind and burst through the stairwell door, ready for anything. Moving quickly up the stairs to the next floor. Opening the door to the third floor slowly. I peer out the crack of the door before making a grand entrance. What I see appears to be business as usual on the floor. A few nurses roaming from room to room, unaware of what just transpired just one floor down.

The sign on the wall shows me the way to the Jacqueline's room. I only need to make it four rooms without incident and then I will be where Jenny told me to go. Moving calmly, but with a purpose, I leave my hiding spot and head to the room.

I duck into the room without being noticed, only to find a shotgun pointed at my head. Jenny lowers the weapon and hugs me. I see Jacqueline laying there, tubes in her nose and arm. The slow beep of the monitor shows exactly how weak she is. I've been hooked up to plenty in my time and know that when her vitals are this low that there's serious trauma.

Mother is waiting at Jacqueline's bedside, holding her hand tightly and mumbling in a language that only she can understand. Sebastian has taken his post near the window, like he always does. The way the big man is gripping his club, I know he's holding back his emotions. Jenny, who was covering the door, is now at my side. I focus my sight and try to look inside of her, thinking maybe I can see something they missed, something that could make her heal faster, but I can't.

Fred comes in the room carrying four coffees. From the pain in his face, I assume he's feeling guilty for not being there. Being on my own for so long has jaded me in more ways than one. I never know what to say in these situations, and I know sarcasm isn't the way to go. I do the only thing that sort of seems right. Taking the coffee from him to free his hands up, I set them on the table next to the bed, keeping my mouth shut.

Without looking away from the window, Sebastian says, "I trust you took care of the issue downstairs."

Walking up next to him, I say, "Yes and no. In a way it took care of itself."

Continuing his eagle like gaze on the parking lot, he asks, "What do you mean, that it took care of itself?"

Quietly, I say to him, "Well, while I was grilling one of them for info, one of his buddies showed up and put a bullet in his head. Then he took off down the stairs."

With a shrug of his massive shoulders, he says, "Through the years, it's always the same with fanatics, no matter their belief. It's better to be dead than to talk. That's devotion I guess."

Shaking it off, I say, "If you say so." I go back to Jenny's side to offer a little comfort.

Holding Jenny, I I say, "Hey babe, I got a question for you."

Jenny looks up at me, and asks, "Yeah, what's your question?"

Unsure of how to ask, I just go for it and say, "One of the guys I was questioning, seems to think that you have a relic. He said someone gave it to you. Has anyone given you something old, passed down family stuff?"

Jenny thinks about it for a few seconds, then says, "An aunt I had gave me her rosary before she passed away. She was a nun for as long as I can remember. She said to always keep them on me and they would protect me. I got them right here." Reaching in her jacket pocket, she pulls out the rosary. The black wooden beads, with a black string dangles from her hand. It looks normal enough, but my knowledge of them is fairly limited.

Mother opens her eyes and looks up at the two of us. Her eyes seem to be focused on the rosary. Mother reaching towards us says, "Bring those to me child."

Jenny passes the rosary to Mother saying, "Here you go."

Running each bead over and over in her hands, Mother says, "You said your aunt gave these to you before she passed away?"

Jenny slightly confused by the question, says, "Yeah, why?"

Mothers demeanor changed from concern and worry for her friend to excitement, as she says, "Well the church must have trusted her, because these are not just an ordinary rosary. These are special. They were made from the true cross."

Jenny, leaning in to get a closer look asks, "How can you tell? They look just like every other set I've seen.

Balling them up in her hand, Mother says, "I can feel the power course through them. They get their color from the blood staining the wood. Jesus as they call him was a demigod as well. He could heal the sick just by touch. Lets hope they still have a little juice left in them." Placing the balled up rosary on Jacqueline's wound.

Nothing was happening at first. It took almost a minute before the monitor begins beeping faster, and Jacqueline's vitals return to normal. Jacqueline sat up quickly, pulling the tube from her nose. There was no way we could explain this to the doctors or nurses without creative lying. Those lies better come quick, because this is sure going to draw attention from whomever is watching the monitors at the nurses station.

Knowing we can't just walk out of here with Jacqueline the way she is in that ass to the wind gown, Jenny digs in her bag for extra clothes. She pulls out a pair of yoga pants and shirt. I'm didn't want to ask why she has a change of clothes with her but I'm going with the theory of me getting blood everywhere. Jacqueline and her aren't exactly the same size but close enough for the clothes to work for the time being. I pull the curtain while the ladies assist her in changing. We make the plan to leave one at a time, with Jacqueline in the middle of the pack. I will go first to draw away any aggression towards me, giving them breathing room for an escape. It's set for the lineup to be me first, Jenny, Fred, Jacqueline, Mother and bringing up the rear is Sebastian. The big guy can handle anything that might try to attack from the rear, and he looks ready for someone to make that mistake.

Changed and ready to go, we line up to leave. Each person will wait fifteen seconds between the next leaving. I throw up my hood and walk out in the hallway. Making a quick left, I walk swiftly towards the stairs. Entering the stairwell, I hear the door open to Jacqueline's room and the sound of Jenny's footsteps on the floor heading my way.

One after another we file into the stairwell. Things start to get crowded on the landing, so I have the others start down the stairs toward the exit. I pass one of the pistols that I took from the last group I encountered to Fred to lead the group down. Sebastian has yet to join us a solid minute after Mother came through the door, causing me to worry.

As they move carefully down, I get ready to go check on Sebastian. When I reach for the door, Sebastian burst through and in a rushed tone says, "Got it, lets move!"

Following quickly behind him, I say, "Got what, what's going on?"

Holding a handful of papers over his head, he says, "This, I'll explain later."

We made it down two and a half flights when I hear a door from above open, a females voice says, "I don't see him, he's probably gone by now." Then the door closes.

Getting to the cars, we part ways agreeing to meet at the diner a few blocks from the book store. Fred takes Jacqueline with him, Mother and Sebastian take Jacqueline's car, while Jenny and I take the one we borrowed from the good officer.

I drive, allowing Jenny a chance to play with the gadgets that the car has to offer. We don't have to talk much when we're alone. This mind reading thing between us comes in handy. We know what each other is thinking and can avoid the awkward beating around the bush crap.

While Jenny is playing with the touch screen navigation on the dash, she says, "Things are changing, you know that right?"

Not taking my eyes off of the road, in a slightly depressing tone I say, "Yeah, I know." I cheer up and jokingly say, "How about after this mess, you and I take a little trip together. You know, disappear for awhile. Just the two of us on the road, with no worries."

Smiling, Jenny slides over next to me and says, "Sounds good to me, maybe we can hit Vegas. I've always wanted to get married by an Elvis impersonator."

Draping my arm behind her, I pull her close and ask, "My, my, Jenny are you asking me to marry you? Because I don't see a ring, and I don't want to get all teary-eyed before waffles."

She slaps my leg and says, "That's your job, ass. It better be something unique."

"You got it. Nothing but the best for you." I say.

We drive the rest of the way, her next to me with my arm around her. We almost seem like normal people. We are nowhere near normal, but it's nice to pretend at times.

Pulling into the diner behind the rest of the group, we park a few spots over from them. I know I don't have to tell her to keep the disappearing thing to ourselves from how straight-faced Jenny got. There was a time and a place for everything and this time is for Jacqueline. Shutting off the car we get out and catch up to the others heading in.

We slide a few tables together and sit. The somber look on every ones' faces tells the story of the day all too well. To most we all appear to be just a random group of people that ended up at the same table. With the recent discoveries, it appears this has been Mothers plan all along. Maybe one day we will get the full story on what the hell is going on.

We order and sit quietly, nobody wanting to be the person to start. Awkward looks pass back and forth between each of us. We all have an ax to grind on who's fault something is, or what could've been done better. It doesn't matter right now, because we got Jacqueline back.

I can't take it anymore and ask, "So Fred, how was work?"

All eyes shift to me and my question. Fred clears his throat and says, "Well, other than getting a message that Jacqueline was stabbed because she was left alone, it was okay. I was hanging off the side of one of the tallest building on scaffolding, how about your day?"

Unrolling my silverware as I see the food going up in the window from the kitchen, I say, "That sounds cool. My day was spent questioning people, setting some on fire, beating some to death, you know pretty normal. Oh Bash and I were loaned this awesome car. One of these days, I'm going to get me one like it."

The look on the face of the waitress must've been of horror, because Jenny says, "Don't worry ma'am, he's joking."

She sets the plates down, and says, "What do I care, that's not the worst thing I've heard tonight."

Contagious laughter starts at one end of the table and works its way around. Now that the mood has lightened up a little we eat our food, joking with one another. The food was pretty good for what it was. It's not like we can go to fine dining. I guess the others could but they might question my appearance., considering that everything I own to wear is either bloody, stolen or bought at a military surplus store.

A thought comes to me while we are sitting here, I wonder if they will miss us when we're gone. Immediately, Jenny's voice comes through in my head saying "You know damn well that they will. Now stop trying to bring me down." I smile at her and blow her a kiss.

We finish our meal and pay. Mother and Sebastian take Jacqueline to stay with them, wherever the hell that is. Fred leaves to crash at Karl's house for the night, leaving the two of us to figure out where we are going to stay. At first Jenny and I consider going to Catherine's place for the night. The place is set up as a fortress, but it being late might risk the chance she's asleep. We settle on going back to Jenny's place and hope for the best. With the amount of people the Twelve have lost, they will want to replenish their ranks before coming at us again.

We take the car within a few blocks of her place and ditch it in one of those pay-to-park areas for the good officer to retrieve after it gets towed. Walking the rest of the way to her house is pretty nice, on this crisp night. The moon high in the almost cloud free sky lit our way.

As we made it down her block, I had forgotten that Sarah had stopped by since the attack. I was half expecting to find the front door still open and the place full of stray animals, but that wasn't the case. The door was closed and porch light on, partially illuminating the man sitting on the deck chair, carving something. Getting closer, the sound of the blade scraping on something that i couldn't make out in the low light, but I can tell it's not wood. I feel Jenny's body tense as we get about ten feet from him. The man sits back, allowing the light to reach his face, it's Cain.

Relaxing some knowing who it is, I say, "Hey Cain, nice of you to stop by, but how'd you even know we would be coming here?"

Still carving, he says, "Simple, I eliminated the options you had and this was the last one. Your place is trashed, the book store is under investigation, the slaughterhouse isn't safe, and the watcher is old and sleeping."

Jenny, walking up on the porch coyishly says, "Yeah, he's a homeless bum and he's all mine."

In a sad effort to defend myself, I say, "Don't forget half Sumerian god and half devil, or is it half angel? I'm not sure, but none of your friends can say that."

Cain puts his knife away and sets what he was carving on on the small table next to him and says, "Are you two done, we have things to discuss."

Jenny unlocks the door, and says, "For now, but we can pick up where we left off later. Come in, make yourself at home." The three of us go inside, Jenny locking the door behind us.

Sitting in the living room, we wait for Cain to explain why he's here. For someone who's been around as long as he has, he seems less than comfortable. Shifting in his seat, Cain says, "I will get right to it. These Knights are one of many people that have it out for you. You need to keep moving, and never settle down, for now that is. While you are still changing and learning your abilities you are vulnerable. Once you are fully developed, the two of you will have no weakness. Any and everything that they can use against you right now, they will. It doesn't matter to them who dies."

Jenny and I look at each other, knowing he's right. I say, "We haven't told the others this but we were planning on hitting the road once we are done dealing with these Templar pricks. Currently, my looks are a bit of a problem fitting in places. There aren't too many people walking around with black rock like skin."

Jenny, running her hand across my cheek asks Cain, "Is there any way other than wearing a mask that we can cover it up? Like a magic spell or something?"

Cain smirks and says, "All that hocus pocus crap is Hollywood bs. There is one thing that I've seen but the ones who control it, don't like to share with those not of their kind."

Leaning back against the couch, I say, "Well that doesn't sound promising. I guess we will figure it out as we go. Maybe I can make a band and tour the world and tell people it's just stage makeup."

Jenny leans into me and says, "Doubtful, I don't think you can carry a tone but the circus might take you." I know she's joking, but that was the next option I was going to pick.

Cain digs into the pockets of his jacket and pulls out a brown paper sack that's rolled up. It looks about four inches thick. He tosses it to me and says, "This will help you on the road."

Opening the bag, I see a stack of hundred dollar bills and a few credit cards. The shock has me stunned silent for a moment, then I say, "Thank you but we have no way to pay you back."

Cain sits back and says, "I have more money than anyone one person can spend so it's no inconvenience. Also I've never found a place that will turn away money, no matter how you look."

Cain's generosity is a hard pill to swallow. There really hasn't ever been a time that someone has done anything for me without at least a few strings attached. Maybe I'm over thinking things, so I ask him, "Why us, why now? I'm sure there's others out there that could use it more than us. Is there anything you want in return, is kinda what I'm asking."

Cain shakes his head no, and says, "I want nothing in return. I'm helping you because we are both outcasts, left on our own to figure things out. They try to tell you that there is some bigger plan, just fail to let you in on what the hell that plan is. They commit atrocious acts and in the same thought condemn you for the same thing. We have to look out for each other."

Jenny sighs. The constant barrage of knowledge being dropped lately is starting to take its toll on her and I both. Cain gets up from his seat, and I ask, "You leaving?"

He fixes his jacket and says, "Yeah, I have a job to do, but you will see me again. You can count on that."

I nudge Jenny, so I can get up and say, "Okay, well I will walk you out."

We walk him to the door, say our goodbyes. Closing the door behind him, we lock it. Jenny waves for me to follow her upstairs. I jog over and snatch the bag that Cain had gave us, then go upstairs.

Jenny was waiting for me in her bedroom when I get there. She's kicking her boots off into the corner and then starts digging for fresh clothes in her dresser. Following her lead, I sit down and untie my boot and toss them over by hers. Standing back up, I peal my shirt off and drop it near the foot of the bed. She walks by me heading to the bathroom when she grabs my belt to drag me behind her. There was no fight from me. She turns on the shower, allowing the steam to fill the room. My clothes were gone be the time she turned around.

Jenny pointed to the shower and said two words, "Get in."

Without hesitation, I was in the shower. The water bounced of my stone skin, the ash from today's activities washed down my body towards the drain. I hear the music start playing only a few seconds before Jenny steps in to join me. I feel my body start to heat up as I took in every inch of her. She had a glow about her that seems to radiate from her the closer she got. My fiery red flesh cools under her touch as she runs her fingers down my chest. The mix of fire and sparks envelope the both of us causing the water to evaporate before it even comes in contact with our naked bodies. Sparks bounce from tile to tile on the bathroom walls during our embrace.

I trace her figure with my hand just off of her porcelain flesh, watching the electricity dance. Turning her around, I pull her hair to the side and lightly kiss her neck. Since my human skin has been shed, she is the only one that can make me feel. As our bodies combine, the power pulses filling the room with a stillness like everything else has been paused.

She spins around, wrapping her legs around my waist. I hold her with one arm as I lean her against the shower wall. Her hands grip the tile as our intensity grows. The flames around us flash melting the curtain to nothing more than a puddle of plastic on the floor.

Feeling the end closing in, I look deep into her eyes and see them change from emerald green to electric blue and finally pearl white. Her body tenses and she latches both arms around my shoulders. Her fingers dig into the meat of my back. With a massive shockwave we were spent.

Our bodies quivering as she unlocks her legs from around me. Weakly she stood, arms still gripping me for balance, not like I was doing much better. If it wasn't for the wall, we would both be on the floor. It took a few minutes to regain stability before we actually shower.

We didn't even bother redressing before clawing into bed. Our energy was drained. This time seemed different from the last in more ways than one. We both are worn out and not charged up. The fire merging with the electricity was new as well. Whatever it was, it doesn't seem to bother Jenny. She just curls her naked body next to me, and we both drift off to sleep.

Opening my eyes, I see Jenny still next to me. The glow of her skin in the morning sun causes me to smile and pull her close. Kissing her cheek, she begins to stir. She awakens, allowing me to see her eyes are a swirling cloud of white. I recoil quickly, and catch myself from the shock.

Jenny sits up and asks, "What's wrong, why did you do that?"

I kiss her on the forehead and say, "Sorry baby, your eyes caught me off guard. I wasn't expecting it this early in the morning."

"What about my eyes?" She says getting out of bed. Looking into her mirror on her dresser to see what I'm talking about. "HOLY SHIT!" she exclaims.

I get out of bed and stand behind her. Leaning down, I wrap my arms around her waist and place my chin on her shoulder and say, "I'm sure they will go back to normal soon enough baby. I noticed them change last night while we were, you know. I didn't think anything about it. Besides, it's kinda hot."

Freaking out, Jenny turns around and says, "What am I going to do? I'm supposed to work today. I can't deliver shit with my eyes looking like a snow storm."

Gently, I grip her shoulders and look into her eyes and say, "I'm sure it will go back to normal, and if it doesn't then you can just wear some sunglasses or tell people they are contacts that you ordered from Japan. They have tons of weird shit over there."

Between her deep breaths, she says, "Yes, glasses. I can do that. Where the hell are my glasses?" She turns back to franticly look through the pile of stuff on her dresser for some glasses to wear.

I walk her back to the bed, and say, "Lets just sit down and relax for a bit, see if that helps. My abilities are always amped when I get worked up."

"Okay, I'll give it a shot." Jenny says.

While she sits on the bed, I go into the bathroom to get our clothes that we never made it into last night. The room more resembles a combat zone than a bathroom with the amount of burn marks from the sparks and flames shooting off of us. All I could do is shake my head and pick up the clothes. I'm not going to tell her about the damage for now, Jenny has enough going on right now to worry about this mess. Cleaning it, gives me something to do while she's at work anyway.

I carry the pile of clothes back to the bedroom only to find her staring into a smaller hand mirror. Tossing the clothes on the bed, I sort them out between hers and mine. I know nothing I do will change what she's going to do, so I just save my energy and get dressed. Being careful of my thoughts, since I'm not sure if she's too occupied to read my mind or not, I play back the events of the last few days. There had to be something missing, something I didn't notice at the time that could be the key to end this once and for all. Nothing was standing out to me. I wish the guy I was questioning in the hospital wouldn't have gotten taken out before he could spill what he knew. He looked like a talker from the way he was squirming.

A thought hits me and I dig through my pockets for my phone. With phone in hand, I do a search for the Renaissance festival website. There has to be at least one picture of the different actors. It only took a minute of searching when I scroll across a picture labeled as the knights of the round table. I recognize two of the guys in the picture for the last couple days. Since those two are dead, they won't be much of a problem, but these others are now on my radar. I screen shot the picture to save it for the others to check out.

I look back at Jenny and see her still checking out her eyes. From her smile I guess they are going back to normal, so I say, "Work or no work, if you don't put some clothes on soon, you're not going to make it on time and more things are going to get torched."

Jenny kicks at me, and says "Not like I wouldn't want to but someone has to hold down a job."

I glare at her for a second, not expecting her quick wit and say, "I don't need a job, Cain is my sugar daddy. Yours too if you think about it."

She sets the mirror down, shrugs and says, "Oh yeah, but if I go in, I can snag us some free food." Then she starts to get dressed.

Once she leaves for work, I text Mother about the eye thing. It's probably nothing more than part of her transformation, but it doesn't hurt to ask. I scrounge through the refrigerator for something to eat while I wait to hear back. It's pretty empty except for some leftovers, so I heat those up and chow down. Mixing Mexican and Chinese food wouldn't appeal to many but for me it works just fine.

After eating, I head up to the bathroom to get started cleaning. The scorch marks come off fairly easily. It's the puddle of melted shower curtain that proves to be an issue. It managed to harden into the edges of the tub. I concentrate on making only my hand heat up and melt the hard to get spots, scooping it right up.

I check the time on my phone and see I've only killed two and a half hours. What's more concerning is that there's no reply from Mother, or anyone else for that matter. Worried my phone isn't working, I text Jenny just to let her know I got our mess cleaned up. She replies within minutes saying she would be home in a few hours. Well at least I know this things working. Now to find ways to fill my time. Well, it guess it's TV and Internet.

Sitting on the couch, Jenny's laptop on my lap, some old western on the TV. I start searching for everything I can think of that might cover my skin. My eyes get a little heavy after a while. I blink, and come to looking through someone else's eyes.

The area seems familiar to me but I can't pin it down. The person is riding passenger in a car. When they look forward, I notice that its a squad car. The police radio mounted on the dash, with the shotgun next to the console. When the body looks at the driver, I recognize him instantly as one of the guys from the picture. The picture had him listed as Sir Gawain. Neither person says anything for a while, just riding along. Finally, the body flips down the visor and looks in the mirror. This body belongs to yet another man from the photo. He played Sir Galahad. Since most of my possessions end with the host dying, I feel its best that I just sit back and watch.

Gawain reaches over and turns down the radio and says, "What do you think the higher ups are going to do since we lost the Captain and LT?"

Adjusting his body armor, Galahad says, "No telling. For all we know they could promote one of us into his spot as one of the Twelve or send in a ringer from Rome."

Gawain sighs, and says, "God I hope they don't send someone from Rome. Those guys that show up from there are pretentious as hell and think they are automatically better than us. We're the ones that hold it down out here, not them."

Galahad shakes his head and says, "I know what you mean. This is our town and we know these streets."

The scanner goes off. The dispatcher says there's disturbance call and spits out an address. It sounds like one that I know but can't put my finger on it. Gawain radios that they are in route, and flips on the lights and siren. He makes a quick u-turn and hits the gas.

I can feel Galahad getting excited as they speed through the streets. I see why as they pull in front of the building. It's my apartment building. As the two get out of the car, Galahad looks towards the door. I see Tim and Fred arguing with an officer. The officer doesn't look familiar to me, and from the amount of starch in his uniform he's probably a rookie.

I hear Gawain yell from behind Galahad, asking, "What seems to be the problem?"

Tim looking frustrated, says, "Your guy here won't let us in the building."

Galahad puts up his hand and says "I got this rook, why don't you just watch and learn." He waves for the officer to move and stands in front of Tim saying "Okay Sir, what business do you have here today?"

Tim getting more mad says, "Well for starters, I own the place. Secondly, I need to get in and get my shit so I can do business. I have tenants in there that need things, elderly tenants."

Galahad points to Fred and says, "And what about you, what's your business here?"

Fred paces, clearly pissed off say, "I live here and I'm trying to get some stuff out of my apartment for work. I'm on my lunch break and kinda in a hurry."

Galahad taking notes looks up and says, "Well the building is under investigation for an incident that happened not that long ago. The other officer is new and just going by the book. It's not his fault. Sir," pointing at Tim, "You go ahead and do what you need to do, just don't go in the room in question. And as for you," pointing at Fred, "Why don't you go on up and get what you need so you can get on your way. The officer is going to go up and watch the unit he's supposed to and not the front door."

Tim didn't say a word, just went inside to his office. Fred, getting his keys out of his pocket says, "Thanks, I can't afford to get docked time for being late."

The moment Fred heads up the stairs, Gawain says to the rookie, "Why don't you go around back and make sure there's nothing going on over there." The rookie leaves and disappears around the corner of the building. Gawain scoots closer to Galahad and says quietly, "I ran the plates to the truck out here. It belongs to one of the people we're looking for. What say we go up and have a talk with this guy?"

Galahad shook his head yes, and asks, "You got that throw away piece that we took off that kid yesterday?"

Gawain jogs back to the car, and says over his shoulder, "Yeah, good thinking, it's in the trunk." Gawain pops the trunk and pulls out a black 9mm pistol. He tucks the pistol in the small of his back as he walks back to meet up with Galahad.

They head upstairs to find Fred. The two officers see Fred coming out of his apartment carrying a tool belt and climbing harness. I can feel the anticipation build inside of Galahad as they approach him.

I know nothing good is going to come from this interaction. The only positive thought I have from these visions is that so far not one of the bodies I've been in has lived.

The look of unease was prominent on Fred's face. He knows something isn't right the way he's palming that blade. I just hope these two haven't noticed it. Locking his door, Fred ,says "Thanks for letting me come up guys. You saved my ass at work."

Gawain, in an attempt to try the good cop routine says, "I'm glad we could help, but since all of us are here do you mind if we ask a few questions? Promise it will only take a sec."

Knowing he was cornered, Fred says, "Yeah, sure. You helped me so why not."

Galahad pulls his small notepad from his shirt pocket. Flipping through to find a blank sheet says, "I see you live across the hall from the apartment that the incident occurred in, did you know the person that lived there?"

Fred shifted his weight, adjusted the harness and tool belt in his hands for a moment and says, "Not really, I know he's the maintenance guy for the building. He stopped by once to say he was going to work on my oven but never showed back up. I haven't really been staying here that long though. Work has me pretty busy and some weeks I'm working out of town on projects."

Galahad nods his head as he takes notes, says, "Okay, okay. This is helpful but.."

He's interrupted by the young rookie stomping up the stairs behind them. As the rookie draws near the other officers he says, "Hey guys, I checked around back and it's all clear. What's going on, why do you have that gun tucked back there, did it come off of him?"

Like it was instinct, Gawain pulls the pistol from his back and fires three rounds at the rookie. Two of them hit the bulletproof vest, while the third hit directly between the eyes.

Galahad shakes off the ringing in his ears and says, "Dude, really? You could have at least warned me. I'm going to have this ringing in my ears all day."

Out of the corner of Galahad's eye, I see the barrel of the pistol. I hear Gawain say, "Orders are orders."

With a flash, I wake. My head rattled and dizzy. I see the reflection of the glow coming from my temple in the laptop screen. It takes me a few seconds to get my composure back, when it comes to me. That son of a bitch shot me. He killed the rookie and me. I need to call Fred.

I dig around for my phone, finding it on the floor. It must have fallen out of my pocket at some point. I scroll through the contacts until I see his name. Tapping the icon, I hear it start to ring.

With a click, Fred says, "Hey what's up?"

I try to calm myself but it comes off more manic than I wanted when I say, "Tell me your okay and you got away."

Now confused, Fred asks, "What the hell are you talking about? I just got off for lunch and have to run by the apartment for some of my tools."

Relieved, I say, "Good, it hasn't happened yet, come by Jenny's house and get me before you go to the apartments. I can explain when you get here, I'll be ready to go."

I'm almost ready to go when I hear the honk of Fred's truck horn blaring from the street. I make my way to the door, stopping to grab my keys and the shotgun off the coffee table on the way by, then out the door.

Hopping into the cab of Fred's truck, the shotgun swings into view for just a moment. It must have been long enough for Fred to notice, because he asks in a concerned tone, "Expecting trouble, are we?"

As I buckle the seat belt, I say, "You don't know the half of it. Head to your place and I'll fill you in." Fred just shrugs his shoulder in a here we go again type motion, and drops the shifter into drive.

I don't have much time to explain, since Jenny lives in the Brookside area of town, while the apartments are at the edge of Westport just a few minutes away. I can see he's uneasy, so I say, "You know how I see things every now and then, right? Well, I just had a vision of you getting trapped by 2 of the cops that are involved in that whole Templar thing. They corner you outside your apartment door. One of them kills the other two cops and that's where I was kicked out of the body I was in. I figured I would come along and help, so you don't get dead and stuff."

Fred's eyes were wide as he says, "Dead and stuff, are you kidding me? You say it like it's normal. Well thanks for the heads up, how are you supposed to help?"

I take a second, and say, "I got a plan, let me off on the back of the building. I'm going to need you to cause a distraction so I can get upstairs. The rest will fall in place."

I can see the worry in his face when, Fred says, "Alright, but your plan better work. I don't feel like becoming collateral damage for one of your half-baked schemes." I can tell he was covering his fear with attitude, but it's better for me to have some sort of plan than letting him go in blind.

I don't even let him stop the truck as we get close to the apartments, when I open the door and jump out. I duck behind a nearby car as I watch Fred's truck make the left to circle around the block. I move swiftly from the right side of the road to the left. Hugging the far side of the dumpster to stay out of view, I wait for my chance.

I hear the arguing start on the other side of the building between Fred, Tim and the rookie officer. Knowing it takes a few minutes for the other two officers to show up, I look for my way in. I see a window on the 2nd floor partially open, just above the dumpster. Scaling the side, I get my balance. Leaning against the wall, I push the window open the rest of the way and climb in.

As quietly as I can, I move through the apartment and out the door. Carefully, I dart up the stairs to the third floor. I hear steps coming from below on the stairwell. I'm not sure if they belong to Fred or the officers so I move faster to my apartment.

Once at my apartment, I go inside and slide into the first door to my right. My old bedroom smells of rot and decay, but I have to remain quiet if I plan on keeping Fred alive.

I hear the jingle of keys come down the hall and stop in front of Fred's door. If it's Fred then I only have a few minutes before the two get up here. As the footsteps get closer from down the hall, I've never felt so nervous. This isn't just my life in jeopardy, it's Fred's.

The sound of the door opening and closing comes from the hallway. Now is the time I should have thought through what I'm going to do.

From across the hall, I hear Fred say, "Thanks for letting me come up guys. You saved my ass at work."

"I'm glad we could help, but since all of us is here do you mind if we ask a few questions? Promise it will only take a sec." Says Gawain.

From here, I can almost hear the worry in his voice when Fred says, "Yeah, sure. You helped me so why not."

The sound of papers rustling, comes off different when I'm not in his body, but I know this is Galahad saying, "I see you live across the hall from the apartment that the incident occurred in, did you know the person that lived there?"

The weight shifts causing the boards to creak in the hallway for a moment as Fred says, "Not really, I know he's the maintenance guy for the building. He stopped by once to say he was going to work on my oven but never showed back up. I haven't really been staying here that long though. Work has me pretty busy and some weeks I'm working out of town on projects."

Galahad says, "Okay, okay. This is helpful but.."

He's interrupted by the young rookie stomping up the stairs behind them. As the rookie draws near the other officers he says "Hey guys, I checked around back and it's all clear. What's going on, why do you have that gun tucked back there, did it come off of him?"

Shoots ring out in the hallway, the first two hit with a thud, while the third causes a splattering sound on impact. That must have been the head shot.

Galahad, deafened by the close range blast, yells, "Dude, really? You could have at least warned me. I'm going to have this ringing in my ears all day."

I get my shotgun at the ready and come around the corner quietly. I see Gawain pointing the pistol at Galahad's head when he says, "Orders are orders." He fires the pistol sending blood to coat the wall next to his partner. As the body drops everything moves in slow motion. I fire the shotgun, catching Gawain in the shoulder and a few pellets hit him in the cheek. It was enough to draw his attention and send him tumbling to the ground.

Gawain rolls on the floor on top of his dead partner, screaming in agony. Fred rushes to kick the gun from Gawain's hand when I stop him. Stepping on his hand with the gun still in it, I put one more round through his head at close range. I send Fred out first to head off Tim and try to explain whats going on as I pick up my shell casings.

Surveying the area, it still amazes and frightens me, the amount of damage that this shotgun does to someone. To think that a month ago I had never held, let alone fired a gun. It seems that if you don't know what you are doing with a gun, that a shotgun is the way to go. No aiming necessary, just point and shoot.

After I check for any signs that we were here, I head downstairs. I round the bottom of the second flight of stairs and almost plow into Fred and Tim. The surprise on Tim's face caught me off guard. If it wasn't peoples reactions I would completely forget how I look.

As Tim lurches backwards, I hold up my hands and say, "Tim, would you calm down. It's just me."

Confused, Tim squints to get a better look at me. I could see he was trying to place my voice with my appearance. As he leans closer, Tim says, "Jacob" in kinda half question/half acknowledgment.

I do sort of a partial wave and say, "Hey Boss, sorry I haven't been around lately. It's been kinda crazy. You know how it is, ancient gods, mythical creatures, secret orders of killers, all that type stuff."

Tim shot me a look of I should stop talking. Pretty much the same look Jenny gives me at least five times a day. Rubbing his temples, Tim says, "Yeah, whatever you say, just get out of here before more cops show up and we all go to jail."

I give him a thumbs up and pat Fred on the back, letting him know its time to get out of here. On our way out Tim yells, "Hurry up and get this shit figured out, you got a lot of things to fix that I'm sure is your fault it's broke. And don't think I'm paying you while you are gone!"

"Got it boss!" I shout back as Fred and I climb into his truck.

Fred knows time is limited, but speeding off will only draw attention to us. Something about just shooting an officer of the law, it makes me want to avoid cops. I doubt that they would even bother hearing my side before they open fire. I'm pretty sure that I could take the raining lead that would be sent our way, but it's Fred that I'm worried about. He must have had the same thought as I did, because he slowed down to thirty mph as he rounded the corner.

I got dropped off at Jenny's house on Fred's way back to work. It didn't click at first, but as I approach the house there was something that seems off. I wasn't gone for very long and everything looks the same on the outside as it was an hour ago, all the way down to the cars on the street. With all these new gifts, I could've picked up a sixth-sense like that bug guy in the comics. There's a good chance that I'm just paranoid from all the chaos that has been flung my way the last few weeks, so I go on in.

Inside, everything is just the way I remember it as well. I mean the TV is still paused in the same spot as i left it. I take off my jacket and drape it over the arm of the couch. I slide the sling to the shotgun over my head and sit the the weapon down on the coffee table. I make my way towards the kitchen to get a drink when I hear the smoke alarm start beeping. The sound is echoing from the kitchen, so I quicken my pace.

I burst through the kitchen door prepared for another fight. Instead of a fight from some unknown attacker, I find Karl. Naked. Dancing. Cooking with headphones in. With all the weird, mystical crap I've encountered and have the potential to come across, this is something I neither expected or wanted to see. Yet, I just can't look away.

The show came to an end as Karl turned to do some spin move, locking eyes with me. He doesn't seem as horrified as I am. He just stands there, a fried chicken drumstick clutched in his teeth, barely hiding his grin.

Karl takes his earbud out of his left ear and removes the drumstick with his right hand. With a full mouth, he says, "What's up, dude? I'm making some lunch if you want some."

A little concerned with his open nakedness, I ask, "You do know that frying things naked is not the best idea, right? Why are you naked in the first place?"

Grabbing an apron from a hook on the wall by the fridge, Karl says, "Well, I spilled my drink down the front of myself on the way over here and threw them in the washer to clean them up before it stained. I wouldn't be naked if someone, not saying who, wouldn't have borrowed my spare set that was upstairs. So I figured I why not make some lunch while I wait."

Nodding, I say, "Makes sense, what's on the menu anyhow?"

Turning back to the stove, Karl says, "We got some fried chicken, fries and I believe there's mozzarella sticks in the freezer we can fry up."

I open the cabinet and grab a few plates as I say, "Sweet, I did work up an appetite. I'll get us plates and condiments."

Karl and I are eating at the counter when Jenny and Sarah walk through the kitchen door. The sight of us must have been too much for the girl, because the turn and go back into the dining room. The dryer beeps and Karl gets up to get his clothes. Left alone in the kitchen, I get up to go join the girls. I find them in the living room talking.

Walking up slowly, I say, "I'm not interrupting, am I?"

Jenny gives me a sideways glance and says, "I was about to ask you the same thing."

I start to massage her shoulders, while I stand behind the couch and say, "It's not what you think. Karl spilled something on his clothes and tossed them in the washer so they won't stain. I was gone when he showed up. I had to take off to help Fred with something. I walk in, and bamm. Naked Karl frying chicken."

Sarah shakes her head and says, "Sounds like Karl. Where did he go anyway?"

Looking over my shoulder towards the kitchen, I say, "Oh, dryer buzzed. So I imagine he went to get his clothes."

Jenny giggles and says, "At least we didn't walk in and find both of you naked."

I lean down, still rubbing her shoulders and quietly say, "Don't act like you don't want me naked."

Putting both hands over her face, Sarah says, "Oh God, you two get a room. It's been a long day and I don't need this."

Jenny reaches over to Sarah and pats her on the thigh, excited she says, "Movie night, lets make the boys watch chick flicks and pamper us."

Sarah drops her hands from her face, with a huge smile says, "Yes! We deserve it and they have no choice!"

I yell over my shoulder to Karl, "Hey Karl!"

Karl shouts back "Yeah."

"We've been nominated to pamper the women while they indulge in a chick flick marathon." I reply in a less than enthusiastic tone.

I hear the sound of a door closing and see Karl pass by the side window in a jog. All I can think is that son of a bitch ditched me. Oh well, I probably would have done the same thing if given the opportunity.

Shaking my head in defeat, I say, "Well ladies, looks like it's just the three of us."

Jenny laughs as Sarah grabs her phone to call Karl. The machine must have picked up because Sarah says, "Nice one ass. Ditching me and now not answering. You owe me big time." Then she hangs up the phone and slams it down on the couch.

The girls went to change into more comfortable clothes and I assume come up with a battle plan on how to torment me, while I clean up my mess from earlier. There's nothing quite like being half devil/ half Sumerian god and being bossed around by your girlfriend and her roommate. I would say oh how the mighty have fallen, but I never was mighty. This is probably the first time I can remember to be living this good, so I might as well suck it up and get use to it.

The girls finally make it back down stairs, pillows and blankets in arm. The grins that they have lets me know that I'm in for a long night. I have the food Jenny brought home dished up and waiting on the table for them. Like a good little servant, I stand waiting for my next order. They pay no attention to me and get comfortable on the couch. Sarah snatches the remote from the coffee table. I can see she's annoyed, but I'm not sure if it's from my presence or Karl ditching her to be stuck as the third wheel.

From her reading the description of the movie she picked, I decide that it's more a general distaste for all men. In the interest of keeping Jenny happy, I keep my mouth shut and sit in the armchair next to the couch.

It didn't take long for the bossing around to start. Five minutes into the movie, I see Sarah and Jenny shaking their cups at me, and Sarah says, "Oh Boy, our glasses are empty. You should probably take care of that."

Biting my tongue from snapping on Boy comment, I politely say, "Yes ma'am, what would you ladies like to drink?"

Jenny snickers, I think she's reading my mind because she touches my arm and says, "Coffee. Yeah, coffee would be nice. Thanks sweety."

Sarah pauses the movie and says, "Sugar, creamer and hurry up about it. And you stop flirting with the help or he will never get anything done."

Seeing my chance to lighten the mood, I say, "It's because I'm black, isn't it? I see how it is."

Jenny erupts in laughter, launching the food she was chewing all over the table, while a flood of embarrassment flows over Sarah. Sarah could barely say the words, as she whispers, "I'm so so so sorry. I didn't mean it like that."

Seeing how Sarah was taking it, I say, "It's a joke, calm down." I reach over to attempt to console her without laughing, but Jenny's frantic laughter isn't helping any.

She seemed to relax and return to normal, so I grab her cup and head to the kitchen. I wait for the coffee to brew and get the cups ready. After filling the cups, I return to the living room. I pass Jenny her cup and say, "Sweet for my sweet." Then I pass Sarah her cup and say "Hope I got it right, don't worry at least its not black. I know how you feel about that." Both of the girls got a good laugh out of it.

With everyone in a better mood, the night went smoothly. I still had to cater to their whims, but at least it wasn't tense in here anymore. I text Fred a few times to make sure he didn't have any other issues throughout the day, and everything went fine and he was with Jacqueline to give her a little protection. Sebastian texts me to let me know that Mother was pissed, but it seems to be more with herself than anything. I let him know that we can meet up sometime tomorrow and get things figured out. Maybe we can move passed all of this Knights bs so Jenny and I can have a shot at a normal life together. Who am I kidding, there nothing normal about either of us.

I wake up in the armchair next to the couch to the credits rolling on a movie I don't even remember them starting. Both girls are sleeping, snuggled up with each other under the blanket. The thought pops in my head questioning if I could take Jenny away from this. She has friends, she has a life, job, the whole thing going. Me all I really have is a somewhat job that I barely did half ass and managed to destroy more shit than I fixed. I need to get out of my own head when I get like this. She's able to make her own choices.

I gently pry the remote out of Sarah's grasp and turn off the TV. Making a quick trip around the house to assure nothing tried to get in while I was out cold. I look at the clock in the kitchen on my through. 5:45 in the freaking morning and I'm awake.

Karl's mess still cluttering the stove and countertop. I do my best to clean up as quietly as I can. Through the window by the sink, I notice a SUV parked across the street. There's a man in the passenger seat with a camera pointing out the window towards the front of the house.

I back away from the window and head back to the living room to grab my jacket and the shotgun. Peeking out the small window next to the front door, I see that he's still there. The plates on the front of the vehicle are government issue. I also get a better look at the driver and passenger. Both men are wearing dark color suits.

I hurry to the back of the house and sneak through the back door. Using the shadows to hide, I inch along the neighboring house until I get to the corner. Lucky for me the people next door don't believe in lawn care, because I use their overgrown bushes to conceal myself from sight.

I manage to low crawl from the bushes to the street and hide next to a van. I watch for my chance and dart across the street while the passenger was looking away from the window. I lay flat and reach under the SUV with my two peeping toms. Pulling up my right sleeve, I focus my energy to make my hand heat up. When my hand is red hot, I grip the first lines I can reach, melting them instantly. I slide a little further underneath and latch onto the drive shaft. The metal heats and begin to glow. Squeezing on the universal joint, it gives with ease.

I slide out from under the vehicle. Gathering the nerve to confront these two, I take a deep breath. I stand straight up and knock on the back window. As I walk to the passenger side door, I ,say "Can I help you guys with something? Couldn't help but notice you out here."

The large vehicle fires up. I hear the driver drop it into gear and hit the gas but goes nowhere. Seeing their horror and disbelief at their speedy getaway being halted, I smile and say, "Awe, you guys having car trouble? Is there anything I can do to help?"

The driver pulls a gun and points it at me. Faster than I could believe I reach in the window and grab the pistol. My hand still hot from a few minutes ago, the barrel warps. I drop the pistol in the passengers lap as he sits frozen in fright.

In a panic, driver bails out the door and takes off on foot down the block. I take the opportunity to pull the one remaining out through the open window. Standing him up, I push him back against the side of his vehicle. Leaning in closely, I ask in the most menacing voice I can muster, "What are you doing here and what do you want?"

In a whimper, the man says, "I was just told to watch this house for a guy." He pulls a picture out of his jacket pocket and in a shaky hand passes it to me.

I automatically recognize the picture of Cain. I hold the photo up to the man and say, "What makes this guy so important that has you snapping pictures of my girlfriends house? What makes you think he's here anyhow?"

The man is still shaking but has calmed his voice a little when he says, "Seriously, I don't know. I just transferred here to this department last week."

I hand the picture back to the man, taking a step back I say, "Go on and get out of here. Just make it a point to stay away from here, okay." He wasted no time with pleasantries. The moment I finished talking he was running. No looking back, no questions, just a flat out sprint.

I walk back up the driveway to the back of the house. It's much too early for this level of excitement. I can't wait for things to calm back down and I can sleep in without worrying about who or what might attack me next. I reach for the door and I here something shift in the brush. I quickly bring the shotgun up, aiming into the darkness.

A voice calls out from the shadow, "Easy, kid. You could cause more damage than you know with that thing." Stepping into the light is Cain.

Lowering my weapon, I say, "That's kinda the point." I step off of the stairs and reach out shaking Cain's hand. "I'm not sure if you know but some of your friends were just here looking for you. What are you doing out here lurking in the shadows?"

Cain looks a little more cautious than his normal carefree demeanor. He peeks around towards the street and says, "Mind if we go inside, I'll explain once we are out of view of potential prying eyes."

I open the door and let him go in first. Once inside, I lock the door and say, "The girls are sleeping in the living room so we need to keep it down."

Cain nods, showing he understands and says, "One issue with being around for so long, is that I've done so much that I can't remember every detail. It has a tendency of catching up with me. This new age of electrics everywhere, tracking everything you do, everywhere you go. With my job wherever I go death tends to follow. I guess someone finally noticed."

Pulling up a bar stool to sit on, I say, "I can see that. Have you tried changing your look up a bit? You know, change the hair, clothes, that sort of thing."

Cain leans against the counter and crosses his arms. He sighs and says, "Over these last few thousands of years I've had every look known to man. It's the facial recognition software that they use now that's the problem."

The kitchen door opens, it's Jenny. She yawns as she stretches. Leaning in behind me she kisses my cheek and says, "Morning babe, what about plastic surgery? Think maybe that would work?"

I look over to Cain and say, "Yeah, that should throw off the images enough. You should give that a shot."

Cain gives off a look showing he's considering it and says, "I suppose it's worth a try. If anything it would be one thing to scratch off the list of things that don't work. Thanks. Do you guys mind if I hide out here for a little while at least until they retrieve their vehicle?"

Jenny shrugs and says, "I don't see why not. Wait what vehicle? I feel like I missed something."

I turn to face Jenny and say in a coyish tone, "You see there were some guys sitting across the street taking pictures of the house and I melted their drive shaft. Turns out they weren't here for us. They were looking for him."

Jenny pats me on the shoulder, turns to head back to the living room and says, "It's way too early for this. I'm going back in there. Someone needs to make coffee and breakfast."

I smack her on the butt as she walks away and say, "I will get right on it baby." Turning to Cain, I say, "I'll get the food going if you get the coffee. She can get violent if she doesn't get her coffee."

Cain and I chat a little more while I make breakfast. I think he enjoys the time to bond with someone that doesn't question or judge him for his past. For me it's nice to be able to interact with someone that knows my struggles. I haven't had that kind of friendship with anyone before. I protected myself to the point of shutting everyone else out. Up until Sebastian snatched me up and Mother came around, I thought it was for the best. Enough of this sentimental crap, it's time for food.

While we eat the room fills with an awkward silence. I had to break that silence, so I say, "Random question time. Cain, do you know if it's possible for someone like me, the way my skin is, to get a tattoo?"

Cain seems perplexed, when he says "Honestly I have no clue. Back in the days where the ones that had that skin were around, tattoos weren't really a thing. I mean body modification through scars was popular and that takes really sharp holy blades. It also looked like it hurt like hell."

"Well, I will just scratch that idea. Not really feeling the getting carved up part." I say

Jenny reaches over and pats my leg, and says, "If you want we can get some modeling paint and do it that way. That way if you change your mind on what you want, just wash it off and do something different."

With a mouth half full of food, Sarah says, "Karl's good with designing stuff, I'm sure he wouldn't mind painting on you."

I continue cutting up my French toast and say, "I'll pass. I'm not going to sit back and let you act like I'm a living paint-by-number."

Jenny shoots me a smile and says, "Fine be a buzz kill. We could have used those for private use."

Cain blushes, trying not to do a spit take.

Sarah's eyes widen as it hits her what was said. All I can do is try not to let the images flood my mind of what possibilities could stem from that. I think some of them are coming from Jenny putting them there telepathically.

Cain and I clean up while the girls head up stairs to get ready for the day. Sarah had mentioned something earlier about working a long shift, and Jenny and I had made plans to meet up with the rest of the troops. Getting ready for me takes no time at all since I don't have much in the line of clothes to choose from. I invite Cain to come with us, but he declines. We warn him that Karl might come by and show him a picture of what he looks like. That way there's no confusion and someone ends up getting hurt.

On the walk over to the shop, I text Sebastian and Fred to let them know we are on the way. Fred said he will swing by later, since he's working till some time in the afternoon. Since I haven't been told not to go to the book store, we continue our walk.

As we are coming up on the shop, Jenny notices first that there is a construction crew replacing the windows. Not wanting to draw attention, I direct us to the alley so we can enter through the rear. It only took two knocks before the door swings open. Jacqueline's reaction of surprise catches me off guard. I was sure that Sebastian or Mother would have told her we were coming by.

There is a strange tension in the air of the store today. I'm unsure if it's because of the workers up front, Jacqueline still uneasy after being stabbed, or if there's something else going on that nobody seems to want to tell me. I feel no matter what the issue is, I need to stay on my toes.

Entering the backroom, I realize what's wrong. We see Mother in a cross legged position, hovering four feet from the floor. An orangish-yellow flame surrounding her in a cocoon. Her eyes open and swirling white. The exposed skin on her arms show the visible scars burning away.

I approach Sebastian and ask, "How long has she been like this?"

Sebastian's face, bleach white from fright, turns and looks at me. In a stuttering voice he says, "About an hour. In all the years I've been around her, nothing like this has ever happened. I went out to get coffee, come back and find..." pointing at Mother, "THIS!"

I take off my coat and pass it to Jenny. I take a few steps towards Mother when Jacqueline grabs my arm to stop me and says, "Don't get too close the flames are burning too hot."

Pulling off my shirt, I say, "Well, lets see if it's still too hot once I flame up myself."

I focus the heat to my upper body, inching closer to Mother as my skin begins to glow. The heat coming from her fiery shell is more intense than anything I've felt before. My skin seems to be drawing the flames away from her and is slowly absorbing its bombardment. I continue forward. Step by step, Mother's eyes regain color. I try to extinguish the flames and cool my own body, with little luck. The fire now consuming my exposed onyx flesh, starts to take control. I feel like I'm stuck in a lucid dream, watching all of my reincarnations pass through me at once. The infinite knowledge of my true mother and father is trying to flow through me. The waterfall of information makes it hard to know what is real.

A flash of Jenny's face, crying and afraid, brings me back to reality. Her voice screaming in my head, gives me the focus and drive needed not to be forever lost. With all of my might I can summon, I draw the flames inward. The fire dies, leaving me slumped on the floor. I can see the scorched wood flooring under my weakened frame.

The blast of the fire extinguisher on my back and surroundings snaps me back. Lifting my head, I see Sebastian carrying Mother's limp body to the large chair near the table. I turn as I stand, finding Jenny holding the extinguisher. She was still squeezing the handle with nothing coming out. Her face reflects the sadness that I had felt in her voice in my head, when she thought I was lost.

Taking a few steps, I feel the charred wood flooring crackle under my feet. It takes me until now to realize that the rest of the clothes I was wearing had burned away. As I get closer to Jenny, her arm goes limp causing her to drop the fire extinguisher to the floor. She rushes to me wrapping her arms around my neck tightly. My skin tingles under her touch, sending a burst of energy through my body.

She pulls back, placing both hands on my cheeks. She leans in to kiss me and stops. Gazing into my eyes, her expression goes from happiness that I'm safe to confusion.

"Your eyes..." Jenny hesitates for a moment, stumbling over her words say, "They're not right."

Disturbed by her reaction, I ask franticly, "What do you mean they aren't right?" The glazed look in her eyes, and lack of response almost seems like she's in a trance. Snapping my fingers to get her attention, I say, "Jenny. Earth to Jenny. Hey, what do are you talking about?"

She tilts her head slightly, squints her eyes and says, "They are swirling."

A relief comes over me, when I say, "Oh okay, sort of like yours did the other day, and like Mothers did while she was in her trance thing."

Still focusing on my eyes, Jenny says, "No, not even close. It's hard to explain. It's like they have a life of their own. Go look in the mirror." She points me to the large mirror mounted to the wall to the left of the curtains.

I approach the mirror slowly, a little afraid what I might find. I look back and forth between Jenny and the mirror. Once I get close enough to it I see exactly what she's talking about. The black and white swirling of my eyes was hypnotic. Both Jenny and Mother's eyes swirled a starry white. Why are mine so different? Why is it still happening, and what was that flame that caused this? Of course the only one here that might be able to answer any of these questions is out cold across the room.

Turning away from the mirror, I check over my body to see if there's any other changes, but find nothing. I call Jenny over to help check over my back for me. I stand at the edge of the room, naked, and afraid of what might be found as she looks over my body.

"There two slits, almost like cracks on your shoulders. They look about four inches long. I don't remember them being there before." Jenny said in a worried tone.

I try reaching over my shoulder to see if I can feel them, and ,say "They weren't there before. Well, not that I remember anyway." I continued to try to reach them for a few more seconds, eventually I say, "Shift over for a sec, babe. I'm going to see if I can see what they look like in the mirror."

Jenny moves to my front, allowing me to see my reflection. She's right, there are two identical splits in my skin on my shoulder blades. She reaches around from the sides and traces the slits with her fingers. A jolt of electricity courses through my body. This was more of a tender painful spark, than her normal touch. It almost drops me to my knees. The electric feeling fades into a searing burning pain. Dropping to one knee, from the intense agony, I feel a pressure build in my back.

I motion for Jenny to move back away from me. I look up to see that my pain has caught the others attention as well. Mother was even coming to, and catching the show.

In a burst of adrenaline I flex every muscle in my body, sending a massive set of black smoking set of raven-like wings sprouting from my back. The span of my new wings stretch out about eight feet on each side. As I stand, the wings fold up, sitting just inches off of the ground.

They moved with me as I moved, contorting and shifting as I step or spin. The weight of them seems like next to nothing, adding balance to my movements. I couldn't help but dance around trying them out. They are an extension of my body that had to be tested. As I spin, I feel the gaze of the others drilling into me. I'm pretty sure its the wings, but it might also be that I dancing naked in the room.

Coming to a stop while facing them, my sense of embarrassment kicks in. The wings wrap my body, concealing my exposed figure from view. The wide eyed, open mouth stares were unnerving. I wish just one of them would say something. I hate having to be the one to constantly break these awkward silencers.

The curtains open, and in walks Fred. Without looking, he says, " Hey people, I got off early so I went ahead and swung by." He glances my direction, with pure excitement, Fred says, "Dude, killer wings. When did that happen?"

His reaction made me feel better about the situation, so I say "Thanks, they kinda just shot out of my back a few minutes ago. Even though they look cool as hell, I'm afraid they are going to make it even harder to blend in with a crowd."

Tossing a chip in his mouth, Fred says, "Well, first step to blending in would be to put some pants on. I'm not even sure I want to know why you are standing here buck naked."

I give a slight nod towards the other, and say, "Worse part is I've been dancing around like this, while they just sit there and watch." My comment makes the other snap out of their creep mode.

Jenny digs in her bag and tosses me a pair of pants and my shirt. I get my pants on and hold my shirt trying to figure out how to fit it on over the wings. As I put my head through the hole and start to slide my right arm into the sleeve the wings draw back into the slits in my shoulder blades, allowing me to get my shirt on. The action was almost instant.

Jenny comes closer, amazed she says, "How did you do that? It's like a switchblade."

Just as surprised as her, I say, "No clue. I thought about it, and it happened. All I know is these things are freaking cool. Think I can fly with them?"

Mother rights herself in the chair, and says, "Those are things only your father would know. They look just like his did after the fall."

Almost in unison, Jenny and I ask, "The fall?" I pull on my jacket and step closer to Mother and say "As in The Fall, like fell from grace fall?"

Mother adjusting her clothes nervously says, "That's correct. I knew him before and after he was cast out. He once had brilliant golden wings and armor. He took up a different appearance when he felt cast out as an outcast. He figured if he's going to be made to play the villain then he should look the part."

Sebastian, steps closer to Fred and takes his bag of chips. Fred gives him a dirty look but doesn't want to test Sebastian. While grabbing a handful of chips, Sebastian says, "I wonder what's going to happen if they pop out while you are wearing a shirt. You might think about cutting a slit in the back of your stuff so it doesn't choke you out or something."

Jenny reaches into her bag and pulls out a four inch lockback pocket knife, and says, "Great idea Bash, Jacob hold still."

A little nervous about the way she's holding the knife, I say, "Hold up, lets cross that road when we come to it okay. We still don't know why they showed up in the first place, or if they will again."

Mother clears her throat, stands up and walks over to me. She places one hand on my cheek and says, "I know exactly why they showed up, my boy."

Anxious for her to go into more depth, I ask, "Well, do you care to explain to the rest of the class please?"

Patting me on the cheek twice, she turns and walks back to her chair and says, "They were a gift from your father. The flame you say me in when you arrived is just his way of communication. While trapped in his own realm, he can still reach out. He found out that you were transitioning and a few of the hurdles you were facing. So in his grandiose fashion, the flames that spoke to me, passed into you. They gave you your new wings along with other gifts that only he knows of. As for your eyes, that's your bodies way of finding its balance, and should return to normal."

Trying to process what Mother just told me, I sigh and say, "Some dads send cards, some call or text but mine uses a supernatural-flaming-portal thing. Why the hell not. Nothing else is normal around here, why would this be any different."

Jenny senses my frustration, and leans in to hug me from the side. I hug her back, and lead her over to the table. I sit and wave everyone over to grab a seat, and say, "Okay everyone, we have some stuff to figure out." I wait for the others to get seated and comfortable. "The other day I had a vision. It was another premonition. This time it was about Fred. Luckily, it turned out okay and the only ones that got hurt were the ones after him. The way the vision went, it looked like they were trying to set him up for killing two cops. One was on the list of people after us, while the other was just a rookie that happened to be in the wrong place trying to do his job. I managed to take out the one setting him up. So that's two more off the list of the Twelve. By my count, I believe we have taken out five or six of them. They seem to always have helpers and I heard them talking about the possibility of Rome sending backup. The way these guys were talking, the out-of-town guys are no joke. Does anyone have any thoughts on how we can get them to back off and go away?"

The blank stares coming from everyone, gives me the impression that they are just as lost as I am. Fred reaches across the table and snatches his chips back from in front of Sebastian, and says, "What if we call the feds and make a report about terrorists coming in from Rome. You know anonymous from a burner phone. They take those thing seriously from what I've heard."

Jenny shrugs and says, "It's worth a shot. I can grab a burner phone later on. I know a gas station that has them and takes cash."

Sebastian a little irritated by Fred taking his chips back, shots Fred a mean look and then turns back to me and says, "Well, that might solve the visiting one but what are we going to do with the ones that are already here? We figure there's at least six or seven top guys left. All we need to do is draw them out together somehow."

Jacqueline sits back in her chair, and says, "Other than walking into the police department and calling them out, I don't know what would get them in one spot."

I sit up quick, almost sending Jenny, who was sitting on my lap, to the floor. I catch her from falling and say, "Sorry baby." I point at Jacqueline and say "That's perfect. That's what I'll do, they won't expect it. They wouldn't dare expose themselves to the rest of the department, especially if we can get the feds in there at that time."

Fred leans forward, resting his elbows on the table and says, "Let me get this straight. You want to walk into the police station and take these guys on, and your only hope is that they aren't crazy enough to go after you in front of others that might or might not be in on it?"

Nodding yes, I confidentially say, "Exactly."

Sebastian's massive chest bounces as he chuckles and asks, "And what is your genius plan to get the feds down there?"

Leaning back, I say, "Easy, they were outside the house last night, watching for Cain. I melted their drive haft, and chased them off. One of the guys dropped his wallet, plus their car is still sitting there."

Mother shakes her head in disbelief, struggling to form a sentence before she says, "Sometimes I think knowing what is going on is important, but then you come up with things that are better if you kept them to yourself. I thought we discussed you talking your ideas over with someone first."

Jokingly, I say, "Hey, it was five something this morning. I thought I would be nice and let you sleep in."

Everyone except Mother tried not to laugh. For Sebastian and Jacqueline, they have never seen anyone talk back to Mother the way I do. For Fred and Jenny, I assume it's because they know I'm going to do what ever comes to mind. I look at it as I haven't died yet, so what the hell.

We plan our strategy down to every last detail. The who's going to be where, the when. The how is another story. Jenny is going to place the call on the burner and charge me up before heading in. Fred and Sebastian are going to stay back with Jacqueline and Mother. Those four don't have any business being around when the bullets start flying, and I'm positive that they will fly.

We take a break from planning so Jacqueline can deal with the repair guys up front. Fred takes off for a few to pick up some food for everyone. Mother still seems a little weak from the earlier conference call from the devil. I give Jenny a nod, and let Sebastian know we are going outside for some air.

The streets are quiet for this time of day, I can only guess it's the time of year. With the fall weather setting in, there's less foot traffic from the hipsters. Behind the shop, I give Jenny a wicked smile and say, "I felt I needed to come out and stretch my wings."

Jenny's face shows her concerns, but I can feel the excitement fuming off of her as she says, "Just be careful. We don't need to get the cops called on us before we do what we have to."

I take off my jacket, and the instant I think of my wings, they slice through the back of my shirt. The tears are perfect cuts the same size as the slots in my back. My smoking black raven wings unfurl casting a massive shadow and amazing silhouette.

It takes a minutes to figure out how to control them before I notice it's by thought, and not muscle control. What I think they do. I finally get them to flap a few times, but I remain planted on the ground.

Furiously they flap, it wasn't until I angled them downward that I feel the lift. Pushing off with my feet, I launch into the air. My concentration goes to being airborne and I forget to continue moving the giant wings, sending me plummeting to the alley floor.

Right before I face plant into a trash pile, the wings take over. Skyward bound, I glide like a rocket. Swooping down, I hug the rooftops of the neighborhood, doing my best not to be seen. The problem is, I'm having too much fun to care.

Swinging around to head back to the store, I spot the contractors that were working on the book stores windows, pulled over speaking to a few cops. At the speed I'm traveling, there's no way I can tell if it's a simple traffic stop, or if they are passing along information on us.

In a rush, I come in for a hard landing. The wings spike the ground, preventing me from crashing. I grab my jacket from Jenny, drawing my wings back into my body. Slipping my jacket on, I motion for Jenny to get inside.

Darting down the hallway, Jenny follows close behind. Turning the corner, we duck into the back room through the curtains. We are barely able to stop as I see an officer standing with a pistol pointing in Mother's face. The officer turns firing multiple rounds in our direction. I wrap my body around Jenny's to protect her. My wings spring out, engulfing our bodies in a cocoon of feathers and smoke.

The rounds are absorbed by the smoke on impact. I push Jenny out of the room as I hear the pistol being reloaded. As I turn to face the attacker, his startled fumbling of his spare magazine becomes more frantic. Sebastian taking the opportunity, swings his bone club into the man's ribcage, sending him stumbling towards the wall.

The officer seats his magazine, raising the barrel of the pistol. I pivot to block any more shots that may be fired. My wing extends, spearing him in the shoulder. I draw the tip of the wing out of the man's shoulder, and with a quick swipe to his throat, his head falls to the floor.

Still not sure how I did it, I stand in awe of what happened. I notice the blood coating the tip of the feathers, smoke and burn away. Drawing my wings back inside, I face the others, and say, "Are you guys alright? Where did that guy come from, we were only outside like ten minutes tops."

Sebastian stands, surveying the bleeding out corpse says, "Shortly after you guys took off."

Jenny moving over to the table says, "Did he say what he wanted, or anything?"

Jacqueline, grabbing the mop bucket from the corner says, "Nope, just walked in, gun out and ready to start shooting. He didn't say a word to any of us."

Mother doesn't appear shaken in the least says, "Probably just another goon for the Twelve that wanted to earn a spot at the big boys table."

I look back at the head to see if I recognize him, and say, "Obviously he didn't have all the details of who he was dealing with."

Sebastian in a chuckle says, "Hell, we don't even know what he have, how would anyone else."

Jenny giggles and catches herself saying, "Sorry, it's true. Between Jacob and I evolving, and all the things we don't know about you guys, there's no way for anyone to have an accurate knowledge of what we have. This could be to our advantage." The rest of us look at Jenny, and she says, "With his new wings that literally just happened as a defense, and my whatever it is power, that none of them have seen yet, we might be able to catch them far enough off guard to take them down without anyone else knowing what's going on."

"Well I'm sold, Sebastian mind helping me get this body down to the furnace?" I say picking up the legs of the corpse. Sebastian comes over and grabs the arms of the body.

We start walking to the basement door with what's left of the attacker, when Fred walks in carrying bags of take-out. Fred sees what we are doing and says, "Seriously, I've been gone about half an hour. This is why I don't take you places."

Sebastian and I look at each other, I nod towards the food and say, "Lunch break." Dropping the body, we go to see what Fred brought to eat.

Fred points over to the body and says, "Dude, you can't leave that there. What happens if someone walks in and sees?"

Digging through the bag, Sebastian says, "Technically, they will see what happens if you just walk in. That's what he did and look how that turned out."

Mother didn't even have to say a word, she just shoots Sebastian and I a look, and we know what we have to do. Reluctantly we pick up the body and heave it down to the basement. While we attempt to cram the limp bulky figure into the furnace, the head comes rolling down the stairs.

Finished with disposing of our unwanted guest, we head up the stairs and wash our hands off. It's hard to enjoy a burger when you know you got dead guy all over your hands. We sit down to eat and of course what's left of the food is cold. I get an idea and signal for Sebastian to pass me his food for a second.

I focus and heat my hands till they are barely glowing. Holding the burgers, I see the cheese start to melt. Pleased with my plan, I pass the big man his steaming hot burger. The looks I receive from the others makes me laugh. What's the point in having these gifts if I can't use them how I want.

We eat and discuss our plans for a while, deciding that it needs to be sooner than later. The longer we wait, the more chance they have to notice that they are running out of help. Jenny throws out the suggestion that we do it right at shift change tonight.

It makes the most sense when to do it. They are all at the station, either getting off or going in. I reach out to Cain to give him a heads up of what's about to happen and to stay away. With the feds on his tail he doesn't need to paint more of a bull's-eye on his back. Especially since we are inviting them to the party. I also reach out to the local field office of the federal officers and claim that Cain will be at the police station at ten o'clock on the dot. Hopefully it will get their juices flowing enough to make them want to be there.

There's nothing I can really do to prepare for what I'm about to do. I'm basically walking into the lions den alone. Sure, I should be all charged up ready to go, but it doesn't stop the jitters. As long as everyone else is safely out of harms way, I care go wild.

The night sets in. The secret safe room is open and ready for Mother, and the others to get into in case something shows up here. I help Sebastian flip the heavy table onto its side and slide it in front of the doorway, providing a little hurdle for anyone rushing in.

While Jenny and I get ready to leave, we lock up the back door, and I drag shelves into the hallway to slow anyone down that breaks in. We leave through the front, locking it as we go out. We get no more than half a block away when a patrol car rounds the corner. It follows us at a distance, but it doesn't appear to be trying to hide or be stealthy about it. He's going to get a shock when he sees where we are heading.

Block by block we walk. The patrol unit is still following. If he paid attention to where he was he would realize we are only a block from his station. We duck just out of sight behind a delivery truck, allowing the officer to get closer. As the car passes, Jenny uses her burst to disable the car. It gives us the time we need to get away.

I look at the bank clock on the corner, seven minutes till go time. Jenny points out the four unmarked cars with the government plates parked on the west corner of the station. I guess they decided it would be worth it to show up for Cain. This is going to be an interesting night to say the least.

Two minutes to go. Looking at Jenny, I start to say something. Obviously she knows what it's going to be and stops me by placing a finger on my lips. Looking into my eyes, she says, "Don't you dare say it. Everything will be fine, and I'll be waiting for you out here. Let's get you juiced up so you can end this shift. We got a vacation to plan."

Placing her hands on my cheeks, I feel her power start flowing into me. I kiss her deeply, increasing the draw of power. My skin glows a brilliant electric blue, coursing with power. Not wanting to leave her weak, I pull back. I take off my jacket and pass it to her, and head to the front door to the station, smacking Jenny on the ass as I walk by.

Standing at the door looking in, it hit me that this is real and most definitely the stupidest plan I've ever had. It may be stupid, but I'm currently the only one in harms way, and that's something. Things go calm in my mind, and the thought of what's the worst that can happen, I could die and meet my real dad.

Flinging the doors open, I lift my leg to take that first step and feel a pat on my back. Looking quickly over my left shoulder, I see Cain standing there. He grins and says, "Did you think I was going to let you have all the fun? Some of those people in there are on my list."

Feeling at ease, I say, "Well, let's do this. Age before beauty."

The sight of the two of us walking in the way we did, had to look like something out of a Martin S film. We stroll in and immediately have more guns pointing in our direction than I anticipated. Who am I kidding, I would have shot me the moment that door opened if the tables were turned.

Since they were just pointing the guns and not saying anything, I took it as my cue to list my demands. I reach slowly into my pocket, pulling out a picture of the Twelve supposed leaders of knights and say, "Okay listen up, if I can have your attention for a moment." Holding up the picture high enough for them to see, I continue, "I'm looking for some bad people, that did some bad things. If you could send them to me, the rest of you are free to carry on with your day. To make it easier for you I will mark out the ones I've already killed."

Heating up my finger, I burn the faces out of the picture of the ones that have recently been eliminated. The expression on all the officers faces as a flame sparks from my finger lets me know that I have their undivided attention. It could also be that I'm glowing like a lightning bug, but they are too afraid to say which.

I pass the picture to the nearest officer and say, "Feel free to pass it around to the others. I can wait for a minute while you talk amongst yourselves."

Hesitantly the photo is passed from person to person. Their faces couldn't hide the fear that was happening inside each hand one of them. The air so thick with tension and anticipation of what will come, that you can taste it. The longer we stand here looking at each other, the heavier it got. I notice the sweat building on the brows of a few of the officers. Their fingers itching to pull the trigger, yet frozen in place by their fear of the unknown.

As the photo makes its way to the last person, I see movement to my right coming down the hallway. Looking over my left shoulder, I whisper to Cain "Get ready, when they start shooting you aren't going to want to be standing there. I got something new to show these guys."

Cain's eyes catch the slots in the back of my shirt, causing him to take a step forward. He takes off his long, black duster and tosses it on the desk next to him. Pulling the antler knife from behind his back Cain says, "Well that's enough talking, there's a few of your names on my list and I'm here to collect." The vacant gaze that is returned from the officers shows that they have no idea what's about to take place. Smiling, Cain says, "Looks like it's dealers choice."

My wings eject outward as the first shot is fired. My left wing swoops in front of me blocking the projectile. I see Cain leaping over the desk, driving his blade hard into the sternum of the closest officer. A young officer catches me off guard and launches the prongs of the tazer into my side. The electricity pulses into my body fueling my power. I knock the prongs out sending a burst of electricity back down the wires, sending the officer to the ground twitching.

My skin burns glowing hot, and the smoke from my wings files the room, concealing our movements. Focusing my sight, I can see the officers scramble for cover to reload. Cain moves through the smoke with ease, instinctively tracking his prey.

In adjacent room, I see one of the men holding an object that's giving off a strange light. It draws me in, beckoning for me to claim whatever it might be. The one holding it must be one of the remaining knights. As I draw closer to the room, I can hear the item call for me in many voices.

I kick in the door, sending an explosion of wood and brass shrapnel scattering through the air. My sight returns to normal, allowing me to see the man with my prize. He stands ready for battle in his black armored suit, white tunic barring the massive red cross. He draws the object of my attention, a gleaming golden sword. The writing on the blade shimmers and glows, moving as if it is constantly telling a story.

The man raises his face mask revealing that he is one of the men from my photo. The man's face shows no fear, only determination. Obviously that blade was special, and he knows it, so I should probably keep some distance from it.

With the limited space in the room to fight, I draw my wings back into my body. I scan the room for anything I can use as a weapon, and say, "If we are going to do this then let's fight like men. You wouldn't happen to have another sword on you I can use do you? Or would you rather me go all fire and wings?"

The man confused at my demeanor, says "My fight isn't with you demon. We are to protect and retrieve the Holy relics. You brought this on yourself by attacking us. It makes no difference what form you take, I will kill you and retrieve what belongs to the order."

Feeling my anger building, I say, "See that's where you are wrong, let me tell you why." Gripping the edge of the desk, I shove it out of the way and say, "First off, one of your little friends left a note nailed to my girlfriends front door with daggers." I kick the shelving unit out of the way next. "Second, you intimidated a sweet old lady." My blood was boiling, yet the man stayed still. "Third, you attacked an innocent woman in her house."

I take a step forward, and watched him tighten his grip on the sword, when I say, "Forth, you attacked and stabbed a friend of mine. What do you have to say about that? Tell me where any of this is my fault again."

I'm standing within striking distance of that sword now. I'm not sure if he's noticed or too distracted but the acting out and questioning I threw his way. He shakes his head and says, "None of that is true. They would never allow innocents to be harmed. You lie demon. You are just trying to poison my mind against my brothers."

I give off a fake laugh, holding my stomach as I chuckle. Stepping another half step closer, I say, "Are you that blind, that all this can go on and you don't know what the hell is going on in your own house? I watched two of your fellow knights shoot a rookie cop in the head. They played Gawain and Galahad in your little circle. Then that Gawain asshat put a round through his buddies head point blank. If I wouldn't have stopped him, other innocents would've been hurt as well."

His confidence wavers, allowing me to get even closer. His grip shifts on the sword as he says, "They said that you did that, they found your prints all over the area. Explain that."

I hold my hand up, letting it cool back to normal. I slowly hold it in front of his face so he can get a good look, and say, "Does it look like I have fingerprints. It's been weeks since I had regular skin on my hands. They were outside my old apartment and could have easily got my prints from there."

The man leaned in looking over my hands, trying to find prints. His brain must have been in melt down as he processes that everything he knew was all manufactured lies. As the sword starts to lower, I snatched it quickly from him. He doesn't seem to fight me, just standing there beaten and lost.

I hear glass break in the doorway. Looking over my shoulder, another man from the picture enters the door with a pump shotgun. He chambers a round and raises the weapon to his shoulder to fire. My wings come out as the man fires. The shot is blocked by the wings, protecting the other officer as well as myself. He fires five more rounds into my wings, hoping for a different result.

He begins to reload the weapon, giving me a chance to turn. I move to attack, when a shot comes from behind me. Quickly I duck, looking back to see the man I was talking to holding a pistol. Hearing a thud from the door, I look to find the shotgun on the floor, and the attacking officer bleeding from his neck.

The armored man drops his pistol and says, "I'm sorry for what problem that we might have caused. This was not my intention. You will have no problems from me demon."

Returning to my feet, I say, "Hey there dude, real quick I'm not a demon. In fact, I'm not really sure what I am. You be careful out there, I've seen what these guys can do when you don't follow their rules."

He nods at me and says, "Thank you, and you might want this." Taking off the sheath for the sword, he hands it to me. Then starts out the room.

Out of nowhere a muzzle flash lights up the entry way as the shot rings out. The splatter of the armored man is contained by his helmet. On pure reaction, I drive the golden sword through the way where the flash comes from. Through my anger, I spin, swiping my wing. It cuts through the wall with ease, metal framing and all.

Rushing out the door, I find a man's abdomen down, still standing, being held up by the sword through the wall. His chest up, lay on the floor at his feet, severed cleanly. His face frozen in terror was recognizable from the picture, meaning that there were only three men left on my list.

I go back in the room to grab the sheath and strap it on my back. Ripping the sword from the wall, I hear the body drop. Sheathing the blade, I venture out to check on Cain and check the bodies for my missing three knights.

The corridor is something out of a horror movie. Blood and chucks of flesh dripped from ceiling and light fixtures onto the coated floor. Lights are so saturated from splatter that it's giving off a red tint to the room.

In the lobby, I find Cain standing near a desk. As I get closer, I see he's stacking the heads of the ones he's killed. A little confused, I ask, "Hey Cain, buddy, what you got going on over here?"

Startled, Cain spins to see me looking over his shoulder and says, "Oh hey, I was just trying to make it easier for you to pick out the ones you might be looking for. How many did you get on your list?"

Looking at the pile of heads, I say, "Well there's only three left to find. Let me look over your collection here. On another note, we need to find you a hobby. Because this right here isn't normal."

Cain not phased by my reaction, shrugs it off and says, "Once you clean them off they aren't half bad to keep around."

"I guess." I say, rolling the heads around to see them all. Finally I find some of what I'm looking for, and say "B-i-n-g-o and bingo was his name. These make two more off the list. There's just one left and he's got to be hiding around here somewhere."

I make my way to the center of the room and focus my sight. Giving my eyes time to adjust, I scan the area for anymore surviving people. I spot a faint image of someone moving around, down the hall. I don't know if it's the walls or the distance that's making it come through so weak, but I do know that I need to find out.

Knowing there's a chance that whoever it is will probably be armed and start shooting the second that door comes open, I step over a few bodies to pick up a shield I saw in the corner. My wings can block some bullets, but I haven't truly tested them to their full potential. I think it's best that I don't push my luck. While grabbing the shield, I see a compact sub-machine gun. Checking the magazine, I find that only one round has been fired. Cain must have made quick work of these guys and doesn't even appear to have a scratch on him. It is kind of hard to tell, with the amount of blood covering everything in the room.

Trying to situate the shield and rifle, I say, "Hey, I got to see a guy about a thing. You're free to hang out here, or you can come with. It's up to you."

Cain looks at his blood soaked hands, and says, "I think I will let you take this one, I'm going to wash up a bit. I might get me a cup of that coffee they have brewing over there, smells great."

"Okay, I shouldn't be too long, hopefully. Remind me later, I got something to show you." Cain replies with a nod. As I walk by, I say, "Also, do you want to grab something to eat later, I've worked up a hell of an appetite."

Pouring his coffee, Cain says, "Sure, I could eat, and if it's about that blade you have slung on your back then I have something you need to hear before you go swinging it around."

Feeling I've delayed long enough, I start down the hallway to figure out which office that aura signature came from. Shield up, I work my way from room to room not finding a single soul. The number of offices quickly depleting, while I'm still finding bodies. I know I didn't kill them, and with them having heads, I figure it wasn't Cain.

I didn't realize there would be this many people in a station at ten at night. The body count is now into the mid-twenties. Seems kind of high, but Cain did say he had a list of his own, and a few of them we didn't even kill. The amount of damage and carnage is shocking to me, no matter how many times I see it. I step over a body here and there. Most of them look like gun shot wounds with a few stab victims mixed in.

With only two rooms left to check, I try using my special sight once more to see how close I am. I don't want to walk into a trap if I can avoid doing so. The dim figure I saw earlier is brighter now, almost blinding.

It's not the man itself that emanating the glow, it's what he's holding, what he's wearing. Through the wall, I can see what looks like plates covering part of his body. I haven't felt afraid of anything up until this point. The feeling has just gotten worse the closer I've got to this room.

I step softly in front of the door, raise the shield, ready my rifle. Taking a deep breath, I kick the door. It doesn't move. Backing up, I aim the rifle down at the lock and fire of a few rounds. Slamming my shoulder into the door, it swings open.

Righting myself, I look over the shield and see a fully armored Knight. The armor plates gleam golden in the florescent lights. He stands regal holding two short swords ready for war. The room has been cleared of everything, like he was expecting this to be the last stand.

Shooting him doesn't seem right to me at this juncture. If he wants to live by his knights code, then I'm more than willing to play along. Tossing the rifle through the doorway into the hall, I say, "Sword to sword, man to man. I can dig it."

The man shifts his stance, and says, "You are hardly a man. What would your kind know of honor?"

Drawing the golden blade from it sheath, I say, "Dude for starters, you've never met anyone like me. Secondly, I gave your people a chance to end this peacefully, and your people attacked innocents. Now I'm going to show you what happens when you come after my people."

Allowing my wings to unfurl, I toss the shield to the side. My skin glowing from anger. It pulses the electric blue through the red tint, as my wings smoke. The man's calm, steadfast act slowly melts away as he stares at my form. The sword turns from a brilliant gold to a blackened and red glow of a hot iron.

The Knight takes a clumsy swing with the blade in his left hand. I block it with my sword, knocking him off balance. He jabs at me with his other sword, nearly catching me in the side. I pivot to the left, punching him in the side of the helmet as hard as I can. His helmet shifts, breaking his face plate. Recoil ingredients from the blow to his head, the Knight shakes his head while keeping his guard up.

I back up, giving the Knight a little room. He removes his helmet, casting it towards the doorway. He spits a mouthful of blood onto the floor with hatred in his eyes. He would be more angry if he found out that my only knowledge of sword fighting came from movies. With blood dripping from his lip, he strikes. A flurry of swings with both hands is raining down on me. Some are blocked by my sword others are blocked by my wings. As his attack slows, I can tell he's starting to tire.

With both hands I swing my glowing red blade downward. He blocks by crossing his blades over his head. Speaks fly as I use all my strength to push my sword down towards his shoulder. The fiery blade seems to be weakening the integrity of his sword, warping his duo. The Knight drops to one knee, holding his defense.

As the Knight starts to lose balance, I continue to push. With his blades failing, I quickly draw back and swipe hard to the side, breaking both of his blades at the hilt.

Unarmed and confused, the Knight gazes at his broken weapons. With my left foot I kick him in the chest, sending him to his back on the ground. I stand over him, looking down at the broken man. The defeat weighs heavy on his face. I toss my sword to the side as I hover over him.   Piece by piece I rip his armor from his body, starting at with his chest plate.

Armor plates are strung around the room, landing with a loud metallic clang. With the last piece in hand, I push off his chest to stand back up. The Knight rolls slightly to his right, grabbing the warped broken blade of his sword and drives it into my side.

Out of rage, I swing at his chest with my bare hand in a clawing motion, ripping through his flesh. My fingers slice through his ribcage and exposing his heart. I grip the beating organ, squeezing. It pops from the pressure. The life drains from his eyes, as I release a roar of anger and pain.

Climbing to my feet, I can feel the broken blade sliding against my rib. My scream must have gotten Cain's attention, because when I turn towards the door I see him standing there. Careful of my movements, I ease my way to him and say, "Mind giving me a hand, this thing hurts like a bitch."

Leaning over to check my wound, he says, "Hold really still, and count to ten. I'm going to pull it out."

More than a little anxious, I ask, "Are you sure I can't just leave it there?"

With his gloved hand, he gets a grip on the blade fragment. Looking up at me, Cain says, "Stop being a baby and count."

Gritting my teeth, I brace myself for the inevitable pain that will follow, and say, "1, 2, 3" Cain rips the blade from my side. "SWEET MOTHER!" I scream.

Cain pats my wound as I take deep breaths to take my mind off the pain, and he says, "Okay, now heat yourself up and heal so we can get out of here."

Wincing in pain, I say, "What the hell are you talking about? That's not how it works, does it?"

Frustrated by my ignorance, Cain shakes his head and says, "I forget some times that you are new to this entire thing." Pointing at my wound he says, "If you heat yourself up to full molten fire thing, it will heal up the damaged area and mold itself back the way it was."

I focus, mustering all of the strength I have left. The black skin starts to glow. Slowly getting brighter and brighter until my entire body is flaming red. As I burn, the pain subsidies. Glancing down at my side, I can see the gash melting together, sealing the opening off. Weak from expending all of my energy, my body cools, returning my flesh to its onyx form.

As I lean against the wall, Cain tosses a pair of pants and shirt that I can only assume he pulled off of a corpse. I look them over, not seeing any rips or blood stains. He notices what I'm doing and says, "Found them in a locker, hope they fit. Can't very well blend in as we make our getaway with you running around naked."

I get dressed slowly, trying not to fall over, when he throws a pair of boots at my feet. As I slip the boots on, I call him back in the room and say, "Hey Cain, come in here and tell me what you make of this armor the guy was wearing. It gave off a bright light when I looked at it in my other eyes."

Cain kicks around the armor plates for a bit, I can tell he's trying to find some distinguishing markings. He stops when he gets to the chest piece. Bending down, he picks the chunk of golden armor up off the floor. The look of worry, comes over him, as he says, "This is the mark of Gabriel. As in the Archangel Gabriel. If he's part of this, a few knights are the least of our worries."

I haven't seen anything shake him in our short time together, but this seems to have spooked him pretty badly. I sheath my sword, and Pat him on the back to let him know I'm ready to go. Side by side, we walk down the hallway. Turning to head to the door we walk right into six armed men wear jackets with the Federal logo on them.

Guns raised, badges out, they stand. I recognize one of the men from outside the Jenny's house. The men are edgy, and understandably so. If it wouldn't have been for Cain and I doing all of this mess, it would bother me walking into this slaughter fest.

Trying to control the shaking in his voice, one of the agents says, "Don't move, put your hands on your head!"

Cain looks the men over and sarcastically says, "Which is it? Don't move or put our hands on our heads."

The agent pulls the hammer back on his pistol, and angrily says, "Stop talking and do it!"

Cain drops his bag and duster on the floor. He starts rolling up his sleeves and says, "I've had about enough of this."

Placing a hand on his chest, I stop him from moving forward and say, "Hey let me take this one." Looking towards the agents, I hold up my hands to show them that I mean no harm and say, "Look, obviously you don't know what you are dealing with. If you did, you would know that only sending six of you was a dumb move. I'm tired, and luckily you caught me in a decent mood, so I'm going to let you off with a warning."

The room echoes from the sound of a round being fired. My head rings as the bullet finds it home on my forehead. The bullet ricochets off of my head, hitting the light just above me, sending glass raining down on our heads. Rubbing the spot where the bullet hit, in a pissed off tone I say, "See things like that put me in a foul mood. In fact, it makes me want to rip off your arms and beat your friends to death with them. But, I'm not going to do that."

Before I can finish my thought, all of the agents weapons fly from their hands. Shocked at what just happened, they all have eyes focused on me as if I was the cause of it. I do my best to not lead on that I had nothing to do with it, but I wish I did. Without warning the agents are slammed against their will along the wall.

I look to Cain, and whisper, "Dude, are you doing this?"

Just as lost as I am, he quietly says, "No, I thought it was you using a power I didn't know about."

A loud whistle sounds, drawing our attention to the front doors. There stands Jenny, arms outstretched. She was doing this. In the excitement, I had forgotten she was waiting outside. Cain grabbed his bag and duster quickly from the floor, as we head towards the door.

As we get to Jenny, she releases her hold on the agents. They drop to the ground and scramble to their feet. I watch the agents frantically search for their guns. I close the doors behind us. I melt the hinges and lock, sealing the agents inside. This should give us a few minutes to get far enough away that maybe they will rethink their next move.

I start to jog towards the road, when I hear Jenny holler "HEY GENIUS!" I turn to see Jenny holding the door open to a running car. I didn't ask how she hot wired the car or where she found it. Some questions are better left unanswered. I get in the passenger side as Cain climbs in the back behind Jenny.

As we speed away from the police station, I get my phone out of my jacket that Jenny had sitting in the seat. I text Fred to let him know that we are on the way back to the store. The response I get back of "hurry" has me worried. I tell Jenny to punch it and sit back, watching the street lights fly by in a blur. My mind is given time to drift and consider the possibilities of what we could be walking in on. Could it be more cops, maybe the feds, or something even worse.

I see the store front come into sight. Everything looked quiet as we pull up out front. The three of us run to the back door through the alley. Fred was waiting to let us in. He seems spooked about something but wasn't saying what. I run down the hall to the back room. There was a strange sulfur smell hanging heavy in the air.

Barreling through the curtains ready for a fight, I find Mother sitting in the large chair near the table. Her face was stern. I can see the anger and hatred in her eyes. Sebastian stands in the corner looking completely distraught. The smell of sulfur and freshly burning wood fills my nose. Not knowing who to talk to first, I say out loud to whoever decides to answer, "What happened, what's going on, and what the hell is that smell?"

Fred comes into the room behind me, patting me on the back says, "Well, while you guys were out, we had a visitor. Your dad stopped by and says hi."

Surprised, I say, "What? How is that possible? I thought he was stuck in Hell."

Mother sounding irritated says, "He feels that he should come say hello and visit while he's in town dealing with another family issue. Three thousand plus years of him not being here and he picks now to just swing by."

Cain makes himself comfortable in the chair at the end of the table and says, "I bet it has something to do Gabriel. We found signs of him helping the Knights. That's all we need is those two going at it again. Last time they fought, half the population paid the price."

Tossing my jacket and the sword to the side, I say, "Well that's just great. I was hoping for a break from this shit for a while. At least the Knights aren't going to be an issue anymore. The feds, that's another story, but they might have learned a valuable lesson."

Jenny hugs me from behind, and says, "I say we all take a vacation for a few weeks till things calm down. Who's with me?"

Fred raises his hand and says, "Hate to say it but I was thinking the same thing. I got offered a spot on one of the traveling crews for a month. They need a few of us to head out to Arizona to help with a project they need finished up. The money is good, twice what I get now."

Cain kicks his feet up on the table, and says, "Well, I'm not exactly part of this merry band of misfits but I'm going to disappear for a while now that the government has started looking for me. I've been meaning to get back down to Brazil." Jacqueline, seeming a little hesitant, speaks up saying "I have been wanting to travel a bit. The shops already closed, so no better time than now."

I look over to Mother, I can see her rolling it around her head. Sebastian looks worn out, so I say, "What do you say, you two? That's five of us for it. Mother, I'm sure you could use a reason to get away from here for a bit, with pops running around."

Mother looks up at me, shaking her head says, "You know what, you're right. I was invited to the convention circuit. It would be a good chance to get out and see if I can find more gifted."

Sebastian shrugs his shoulders and says, "Hell, why not. I could use a break from you assholes for a while. Although, I will miss the free food."

Clapping my hands once in excitement, I say, "Alright, other than the asshole comment, I think we are all on the same page. I'm hungry, so I'm going to get something to eat and head to the house to crash. You guys are welcome to join us for food if you want."

We all load up in separate cars to go get food and make our way out to the diner. The streets seem quieter than usual. It could be the lack of cops out. It could be the sign of something big to come, the calm before the storm sort of thing. For all I know, it could mean absolutely nothing. I'm not psychic after all. Well, not that I know of anyway. I think during this break, Jenny and I should text our limits. It can definitely come in handy since we don't know what's next in store for us.

Filing into the diner, and sliding a few tables together, I smile at how our family has grown over such a short time. We order and throw around a little small talk. Mother talks about the old days on the psychic and gypsy circuit.

Sebastian brags about his days as a prize fighter. Cain goes into a little too much detail of how he once took out an entire civilization. It was some place called Roanoke, or something. Fred tells us that his band has a show tomorrow with a few touring bands out of New Mexico. Jenny thinks it will be a good time, and that we will come see them play before we head out for wherever we end up.

After we eat, everyone goes their own way. I let Fred know that we will see him the next day at the show. Jenny and I leave the car that she stole earlier in the diner parking lot and walk home. Even though we just killed an entire shift of officers, there will most likely be someone out looking for it eventually and I would rather not have it sitting at the house.

Once home, or her home at least, mine is still a crime scene, we get comfortable. It doesn't take long to get to sleep. With her next to me, it's easy to drift off. The dreams come on fast. They aren't my normal dreams of others peoples lives or past lives of my own, but animalistic in nature.

I drift from animal to animal but they don't act like the feral creatures that you see on TV. I can feel there thoughts, hear them think and it's human style thinking. When the creature stops to drink from a creek, I catch its reflection. It's a reflection of a wolf, a wolf with human eyes. I think it knows I'm here by the way it stares. That all is stopped, a growl comes from behind the wolf. Something pounces on top of the wolf, pinning it to the ground. With a quick pinch in the neck, I wake up.

Sitting up in bed, I notice Jenny is still sleeping. I don't feel like I can get back to sleep right away. I grab my phone from the dresser and do a few web searches on dreams to see what I come up with. All the pages that come up relate to werewolves and shape shifters. I think if any of that stuff was out there Mother or Cain might have mentioned it by now. I don't remember Mother saying that was one of the gifts that were bestowed on her subjects or whatever she called them. I'm probably reading too much into it and should try to get some sleep. Laying back down, I cuddle up to Jenny and I'm out.

I wake up to the smell of coffee. I find a cup sitting on the edge of the dresser waiting for me. I pull on a pair of pants and a shirt. With my coffee in hand, I make my way downstairs. I find the TV on and a map of the country laid out on the table. I'm not going to worry about that just yet, not while I smell food in the other room.

Opening the kitchen door and seeing Jenny in there cooking away is a hell of a lot better than when I saw Karl. That image is going to haunt me till I die. Jenny has an amazing mix of Lily Munster and June Cleaver thing going on right now. I watch her for a minute while I drink my coffee, and think of how lucky I am.

In the middle of taking a sip, a dish rag flies and lands on my face. She looks at me and says "Are you going to stand there and day dream or help? I don't know where you think you are to get hotel service, but we have a lot of things to figure out before we hit the road."

Setting my cup down, I ask, "What would you like me to do baby?"

As she flips the pancakes, she says ,"I don't know, get some plates or something."

We get the food dished up, and go back to the living room to eat. Jenny is telling me about a few places she wants to visit while we are out on our little road trip. She is telling me about a few festivals that she has heard about, where someone like me could walk around and no one will even bat an eye at. It sounds great, but from what Cain has told me the living fast and wild gets old after a while.

I explain to her we can do and go to those places as long as we take time for ourselves as well. How I want to see what gifts we have not discovered yet. Maybe there are some things that her and I combined can do together.

We must have talked for hours, when I get a text from Fred saying that the show is starting at six instead of eight. It's in some new venue is under an existing bar. I guess it's only used for black metal shows or something. Jenny thinks I should do corpse paint, since it will hide the onyx skin. It's not a bad idea, but she's going to have to put it on me. I've seen a few bands with theirs on but don't really know what flies a correct application.

The plan to hit the road after the show seems to be a go. We have our bags packed, car rented and even delivered to the house. Thankfully, Jenny has an actual bank account to do things like that. I get the car loaded up, while she finishes up getting ready to go.

I check the time as she comes out of the house, finally ready to go and see that we have fifteen minutes to get to the venue. I toss her the keys, letting her drive to the show. She delivers all over this city and might know a short cut there, and if we're late I can blame her. It won't matter, I know it will be my fault.

Getting to this secret venue is almost as much of an adventure as some of the other things I've had to do lately. We went in one bar, then are lead downstairs. Then we go through a door and follow an underground tunnel as it twists and turns. Eventually we come through a small entryway and into an open area. It's cramped and crowded with people. Lucky for us the music hasn't started, giving us a chance to move closer to the front.

The face paint was a good idea. There must be twenty other people with theirs painted. The lighting is dim in here, but it's good enough to be able to move without running into a wall. They have one of those roll away bars tucked in the corner. I want a drink to calm my nerve, but with us hitting the road in few hours, it's probably not the best thing for me.

The first couple bands are locals. They all play and kill it. I originally thought this was going to be an diy show with bad sound, but it actually works well with that it is. The first touring band was a black metal Navajo band that called themselves Changling. They apologize to everyone if they have some issues. I guess that one of the members couldn't be here tonight because of a medical problem.

As they play, something familiar waves over me. It's their sound, an animal instinct feral tone. I can't shake the feeling that I've dealt with these emotions that they are bringing out of me. The lights flicker the faster they play. In the flashes, I see what looks like a few of the members transforming between human and wolf. The guy next to me mentions that he thinks the lighting program is outstanding how it plays with your mind.

I make my way to the bar. I may not be able to drink, but I can give my eyes a rest from the strobes. I see a cooler set to the side with a stack of cups for water. I get a cup an fill it, drinking it down quickly. I go to fill it a gain, and get tapped on the shoulder.

Turning, I see a someone that doesn't exactly fit in in this crowd. He was tall and stocky and sporting a nice suit. The black on black suit was clearly a custom job. The man points at the water cooler and asks, "May I?"

I scoot to the side, a little thrown off by his appearance I say, "Yeah, sorry. It's all you."

The man gets a cup, looking at me while he fills it and says, "Pretty interesting venue isn't it? Do you come here often?"

Drinking this cup of water slower than the last, I say, "First time actually, but I dig it. Kind of has a cult or catacombs thing going for it. How about you?"

He takes a sip, then looks towards the stage and says, "First time as well, I don't get out much. The music is good though. It speaks to me in a way most music doesn't."

I scan the crowd to see if I can find Jenny, and say, "I can see that, it's kinda on the primal side. I could just do without the light show. It plays tricks with your eyes."

He nods and says, "Primal, that's one way to put it. Well, I have to be running. I have some family business to take care of, but you take care of yourself Jacob."

Half paying attention, I say, "Alright, you do the same." Catching what he said, I quickly turn towards him and say, "Wait, what? How'd you know my name?"

With a smug smile, the man looks me dead in the eyes and says, "Easy, it would be wrong for a father not to recognize his own son." With a puff of smoke he was gone, leaving nothing more than the smell of sulfur lingering in the air.

Awestruck and confused, I stand there for a moment lost in what just happened. As my thoughts clear, I hurry through the crowd to find Jenny. She has to know about this.

I find her with Fred, Karl and Sarah to the left of the stage area. I slow my breathing to collect my thoughts so the words don't come out jumbled and say, "You will never guess who dropped in just a minute ago."

The four of them look around the room for a second and Jenny asks, "Who?"

As serious as I have ever been, I say, "Dad!" Fred and Jenny's eyes widen in shock.

Karl, must not have been let in on the family lineage, because he asks, "So what's so bad about that? Is your dad somebody special or just another struck match like you?"

Fred leans in closer to Karl and says, "You can say that. His dad is Lucifer."

Karl got excited and screams, "As in first of the Fallen? That Lucifer?"

I nod yes and say, "Yes, the one in the same."

We talk a little more about it as the band Changling tears down their equipment to make way for the next band. While we stood there the guitar player seems to keep watching me. Jenny notices it as well, because I hear her inside my head say so.

With the last of their gear out of the way and the next band starts to set up, the sense of uneasy is starting to let up. The members of Changling walk back into the room, and head towards the bar. The guitar player passes too close to me, bumping my shoulder. When I turn to ask what his problem is, the man slides a note into my hand and walks off swiftly.

I turn back to my friends and open the note as I say, "I'm not sure what his problem is but he slipped me a note."

Jenny, trying to look over my shoulder asks, "What's it say?"

I hold my phone over the note for light and say, "It says. We were told that you could help us by Cain. One of ours is missing. I will call with more details when I know we aren't being watched."

Look for the continuation in Visions of Change

Made in the USA
Middletown, DE
26 September 2021